VARIATIONS

CLAIRE LORRIMER

VARIATIONS
COLLECTED
SHORT STORIES

BANTAM PRESS

LONDON · NEW YORK · TORONTO · SYDNEY · AUCKLAND

TRANSWORLD PUBLISHERS LTD
61–63 Uxbridge Road, London W5 5SA

TRANSWORLD PUBLISHERS (AUSTRALIA) PTY LTD
15–23 Helles Avenue, Moorebank, NSW 2170

TRANSWORLD PUBLISHERS (NZ) LTD
Cnr Moselle and Waipareira Aves,
Henderson, Auckland

Published 1991 by Bantam Press
a division of Transworld Publishers Ltd
Copyright © Claire Lorrimer 1991

A catalogue record for this book is available from the British
Library
0593 02429X

Typeset in 11/13pt Baskerville by
Chippendale Type Ltd., Otley, West Yorkshire.
Printed in Great Britain by
Biddles Ltd, Guildford and King's Lynn.

INTRODUCTION

Although most of my time is spent writing books, there have been numerous occasions when, perhaps even in the middle of a long family saga, an incident has occurred which has sparked an idea for a short story. THE GARDEN was written when I was recuperating from a near-fatal car accident one summer, and whilst confined to bed, I could hear my children playing in the garden and longed to be well enough to go out and join them. A TRUE STORY was indeed true, whereas THE ANGEL AND THE WITCH was entirely imaginary.

Now that so few women's magazines publish short stories and because I believe very many people, like myself, favour them for bedtime reading, I have collected, from the hundreds I have written, some of my favourites for *Variations*.

C.L.
1991

CONTENTS

The Snake Belt

It all began that February of 1930 when Letty was six.

'Miracles are always possible provided you have sufficient Faith!'

The latent excitement in Sister Bernadette's voice as she made this pronouncement woke Letty from a pleasant day-dream involving a tree-climbing adventure with her cousin, Christopher.

After two terms at the Convent of the Sacred Heart, Letty knew about Faith. It was believing in God, which she certainly did, although she was still confused about there being three of Him – Father, Son and Holy Ghost. She didn't like ghosts and preferred not to think about getting confirmed when she was older because, if you hadn't seen the Holy Ghost before, you were bound to have it descend on you at the ceremony. Nor was she sure if she liked God who, so Sister Bernadette often warned her class of six year olds, had an All-Seeing Eye; which meant that even if no one else saw you stick out your tongue at another girl or laugh when one of the nuns tripped over her habit, God would see and in due course, mete out a suitable punishment. Nor was she all that happy about God the Son: poor Jesus, whose body hung on innumerable crosses in church and in the convent passages, horrible drops of blood pouring from his head and hands and dripping down his body. Sister Bernadette said he died on the cross to

11

save people but he looked to Letty as if he needed saving himself.

'Please, Sister, what's a miracle?' she asked.

'Quite simply, Letitia, it is a superhuman event; which is to say that ordinary mortals like ourselves cannot achieve the impossible. God, however, can do anything and everything if He thinks fit, and we need only have sufficient Faith in His power and pray and He will perform miracles for us.'

Letty's face turned pink with excitement. She had almost – well nearly almost – given up hope of getting the snake belt. Christopher had one threaded through the loops of his shorts. Sometimes, if she gave him a toffee or let him borrow her Sorbo ball, he would allow her to wear it but never for long because without it, his shorts fell down. Letty had begged and begged Mummy to buy her one, or to allow her to save up her pocket money and buy one for herself. Every time she brought up the subject, Mummy explained that girls wore dresses and snake belts were for boys' trousers and would look very silly on a dress. Letty had asked Father Christmas to bring her one but he never did. 'It'll be a miracle if you ever get one!' said Mrs Banbury, the daily. 'So if I was you, I'd forget the dratted thing!'

Now, according to Sister Bernadette, she had only to pray, with sufficient Faith of course, and she would have a snake belt. Would God send it by the postman? Or would it come in her Christmas stocking? Or would God just deposit it on the end of her bed whilst she was asleep? Maybe her Guardian Angel would bring it. Maybe . . .

'Letitia, you are not paying attention again . . . '

12

'Oh, I am, truly I am, Sister!' Letty gasped.

'Then kindly repeat the story of the loaves and . . .'

The bell rang for the end of the lesson and as she left the classroom, Letty decided that the All-Seeing God knew she had been concentrating on Him and shown his goodwill by getting the bell rung early and saving her from yet another detention. A little miracle – but a miracle nonetheless.

Letty prayed. Silently, fervently, continuously she prayed; throughout meals, throughout lessons, throughout netball, before she went to sleep and when she woke up. Most of all she prayed in the big candlelit church, forcing herself to look at the poor, bleeding Son of God instead of at the gentle, smiling statue of his mother, Mary, in her pretty blue mantle, where Letty usually fastened her gaze.

For two whole weeks, Letty prayed. She described the snake belt in great detail to God – the stretchy elastic it was made of, its stripy green, brown and grey colours, the two shiny snake heads which linked around each other so cleverly. She explained that the colours weren't so important and it didn't have to be exactly the same belt as Christopher's and would God be kind enough to leave a note for Mummy saying it was all right for her to wear the belt even though she was a girl.

Either God wasn't listening, Letty decided, or, more probably, He simply couldn't hear her. She decided to get up in the night and pray when the dormitory was quiet and everyone was asleep.

Letty, too, was asleep when Sister Bernadette found her still kneeling by her bed. Only partially

13

coherent between her sobs once woken, Letty failed to make the elderly nun understand the importance of the snake belt or, indeed, what it was.

'Our Good Lord would not want you to miss your sleep, child.' Sister said, adding comfortingly, 'You must never lose your faith, Letitia. In His own good time, God will answer your prayers. Faith, you know, can move mountains!'

Letty didn't want to move mountains but in the morning, she woke up with an idea. Maybe the gift of a snake belt wasn't important enough, big enough, for God to be bothered about it. If he liked moving mountains then perhaps he wanted something more spectacular for His miracle; something like changing her from a girl into a boy who could wear a snake belt. Daddy had said it couldn't be done; that she'd just have to accept the fact that he had wanted a little girl and he loved her as she was.

Such was Letty's faith that she knew God could do the impossible.

'God does not always answer our prayers, Letitia,' Sister Bernadette said when three weeks later, Letty could see no sign that she had been changed into a boy and hope, along with Faith, was draining away. 'God created you a little girl because that is what He chose for you to be. He has His own purpose. At one time in my childhood, I, too, wished I had been born a boy but when I grew up, I realized God's purpose – I was to become a nun and dedicate my life to Him. Perhaps this is His intention for you, child.'

'But how will I know?' Letty asked, comforted and even a little excited to think that God had

14

singled her out for special honours; despite the fact that she was frequently naughty and always in trouble for day-dreaming. She told fibs, too, although not always on purpose. Sometimes she just became confused between the stories she made up in her head and real things.

'God will call you in His own good time!' Sister Bernadette said. 'You will hear His voice.'

Her problem, Letty decided, had done an abrupt turnabout. It was no longer a matter of God hearing her but of her hearing God. She endeavoured to sit in class beside a window because she would be nearer the sky. When she went to the lavatory, she stood by the skylight listening, because it was the only place in the school where it was quiet. She stopped talking to her friends and, once she was home for the holidays, she barely spoke to her parents.

'Is the child ill?' Daddy asked, looking worried. 'She usually talks the hind leg off a donkey!'

'Is something worrying you, Letty?' Mummy asked.

'I'm only listening,' Letty said vaguely. 'I just wish people wouldn't make such a noise.'

Mummy took her to the doctor who said she was a little tense but he could find nothing wrong with her.

'Listening for what?' Christopher asked when he came to stay for a week. He was a year older than Letty and she adored him. He enjoyed her adoration and her willingness to join in any game of his choosing. Letty told him about Faith and Miracles and The Call. For once, Christopher did not support her.

15

'It wouldn't be much fun being a nun!' he said. 'You couldn't climb Mount Everest or sail across the world in a dinghy or fly a hot air balloon or anything. I thought you were coming with me when we grow up. I don't want to take a silly old nun with me and that's that.'

It certainly altered Letty's perspective. Sharing Christopher's adventures was what she wanted most in the world — even more than being a boy and wearing a snake belt. For the rest of the holidays, she only listened for The Call when she had nothing else to do.

'Letty seems much better!' Daddy said. 'More her old self!'

Letty sat in the classroom thinking about going over Niagara Falls in a barrel with Christopher when Sister Bernadette started talking about Limbo . . . a place which was neither Heaven, Hell nor Purgatory. It was, she said in hushed tones, a place where the poor souls went who had not been baptized. Babies went there if they died soon after being born and had not been baptized by a priest. There they stayed, unable to go to Heaven like everyone else.

'Even though they're too little ever to have been naughty?' Letty asked in a shocked voice.

'I'm afraid so,' said Sister Bernadette. 'It is very sad. But you can all help these tiny, innocent souls to find their way to Heaven. You have only to say the sacred names of our blessed Jesus, Mary and Joseph to release a tiny soul to Heaven.'

Letty was enchanted — and at the same time horrified. It was wonderful to think that she — not yet seven years old — had the power to save babies

16

from horrible old Limbo, but shocking to think of the hundreds and thousands which might not be saved. She resolved not to waste a further moment and began at once to chant under her breath, 'Jesus, Mary, Joseph; Jesus, Mary, Joseph.' She had managed to save thirteen babies before Sister Bernadette cut her short.

'Letitia, you are day-dreaming yet again. You will remain behind after the lesson.'

Letty found that with practice, she could save time by shortening the sacred names. Jesus, Mary and Joseph became Jeez–May–Joze. In this way she could say them forty times a minute. She decided that the numbers were too large for her to work out and asked one of the older girls to do the multiplication for her. Thus she learned that she could save two thousand four hundred babies if she could keep going for an hour; that if she could manage four hours a day, she would save nine thousand six hundred babies and, if she could keep this up for a year, three million five hundred and four thousand babies could go to Heaven who would not otherwise have got there.

These astronomical numbers were beyond Letty's comprehension but the senior girl had written them down for her on a piece of paper and at the first opportunity, she asked Sister Bernadette if there might be more than three million babies in Limbo. Sister Bernadette seemed surprised and told Letty not to worry about numbers. But how could she stop worrying, Letty asked herself, remembering just one wailing baby she'd seen in a pram in the park last holidays.

'Letty's looking peaky again,' Daddy said when

she returned home for the summer holiday. 'If you've anything to say, Letty, speak up please. I don't like all this muttering!'

'But it takes too long . . . ' Letty tried to explain but Mummy said Daddy wanted to listen to the news and not to bother him now. The doctor thought she needed a tonic, but Mummy said a fortnight by the sea where Christopher lived would probably put some colour back in her cheeks.

Letty asked Christopher if he knew about Limbo.

'We don't learn about places like that at our school,' he said. 'Anyway, if those babies hadn't got mothers and people to look after them, they'd die anyway. I should think your nun was making it all up to keep you out of mischief. Grown-ups are always thinking of ways to keep us out of mischief. Let's go down to the beach and swim. I've got a new swimming costume now I'm at my new school. I've got all new uniform. I'll show it to you if you like.'

Letty agreed it was very smart, especially the scarlet blazer with the black braid and gold buttons.

'But that's not my bestest,' Christopher said, opening his dressing-table drawer. 'How about that!' He dangled in front of Letty's face a scarlet and black snake belt and watched with satisfaction the look of admiration and envy that spread over Letty's face.

'It's beautiful!' she said with all the enthusiasm he could have wished for. He felt kindly disposed towards her and said generously, 'Here you are, Letty – you can have my old one. I don't need it any more. That is, if you still want it . . . '

18

Letty could only nod as she fastened it round her waist. Her small hands linked the snake heads ecstatically. It was hers – for ever and ever, to wear whenever she pleased; to take to bed with her, to wear under her pyjamas and silly girls' dresses.

'I'll wear it over my bathing suit,' she announced when she could speak.

'It'll get wet, silly!' said Christopher. 'Come on now, we're wasting all the afternoon. Bet I get down to the beach before you.'

It was only as she ran down to the water's edge where Christopher was already splashing his feet, the snake belt securely around her small waist, that Letty paused. A point of enormous importance had struck her. Even if Sister Bernadette was wrong about Limbo and even if she had been wrong in thinking that God would call her, Letty, to be a nun, she had been right about the thing that really mattered. 'God works in mysterious ways,' she had said. Sister Bernadette had never met her cousin so how could she possibly have known – any more than Letty could have guessed – that He would use Christopher's new school uniform to give Letty her miracle?

One in Three

As I left the Customs Hall behind me and pushed my trolley through the doors into the meeting area, my eyes searched the crowd milling up against the metal railings of the barrier. There was no sign of Patti.

'If there's no one there to meet you, take a taxi!' she had said. 'It isn't far!' So I walked to the end of the railings where a group of drivers stood holding up their cards. My name was not on any of them.

My depression deepened. I was not looking forward to the interview facing me this afternoon. In fact, unless it had been imperative, I would not have come back to England at all.

The crowd round the barrier had thinned slightly, but there was still no one to meet me. I thought they just might have been delayed, so I'd give it ten minutes and then I'd go and find a taxi.

I found a group of chairs where I could keep an eye on the barrier. A young woman came towards me wearing the uniform of an air hostess. Very attractive, I thought – and then I noticed the small boy she was holding by one hand. She dumped him in the empty seat beside me, saying, 'You can wait here for me, Paul. I'm going to telephone your mother to say we'll be late back. We don't want her worrying. There's a flight due in from Spain in half an hour. If your father isn't on it, we'll go home.'

The boy's eyes followed the trim figure as his companion walked over to the bank of pay phones. As usual, there was a queue. He turned his head to stare at me and for a moment, I thought he had recognized me. He returned my smile with that English shyness I had all but forgotten. In Spain, children of all ages would converse with you unabashed if given half a chance. At first, I had been fascinated by their large, liquid brown eyes but gradually I took them for granted – just as I took for granted the brilliance of the sun, the violence of the colours, the unlimited variety of subjects to paint.

England in November was not a welcome alternative. But for the fact that a London gallery had offered to give me an exhibition, I would not be here, despite my wife's recent letter demanding I return home to discuss what she called 'an amicable divorce'. Here I was, aiming to kill two birds with one stone and utterly shaken to find myself sitting next to the son I had not seen for three years. There was no mistaking him – he looked exactly like his mother.

Paul had been little more than a toddler when I'd gone to live in Spain – blue eyes in a plump face, hands and knees still slightly dimpled. Now he was a thin, lanky little boy with bony wrists and knobbly knees. He was very clean – unnaturally so for a six year old. He'd probably been spruced up for the occasion. Who, I wondered, was his companion?

'Your air hostess is very pretty!' I said.

'Yes, and she's nice, too. She flies all over the world. I'm going to be a pilot when I grow up.

Janie says I'll have to work hard and pass all my exams. She lives next door to us.'

He was surprisingly articulate for his age.

'I'm not supposed to talk to strangers!' he added by way of an afterthought.

I wanted to tell him then that I wasn't a stranger – I was his father, but somehow I wasn't yet ready for the emotional consequences. I had not expected to be so . . . so moved. As a baby, he'd looked like me – or so everyone had said. Now he was so like his mother that it brought back memories I thought I had forgotten. Suddenly the past had come so close, it reached out and touched me, as if it was trying to hold me.

I had not come home to be chained again to that old torture of quarrelling with Patti; of hating and loving her; of hating myself. I was not in the least surprised that she wanted a divorce. We'd been separated so long, our lives had drifted apart. She had written from time to time, mostly with news of Paul. The letters were always impersonal, unemotional and I replied in the same vein.

At first, it hadn't been easy to sell my paintings, but gradually I found good outlets and I was able to send money home. I owed Patti that, for when I'd left we'd been heavily in debt. Patti wrote that her mother had come to live with her so that she'd been able to return to work. The money she earned together with what I sent, made it possible for her to take out a mortgage on a tiny cottage in the country not far from Gatwick Airport.

In those early days after I'd walked out, I wasn't sure whether Patti welcomed my departure or not.

25

All she had said when I told her I was off to Spain, was, 'When will you be back?'

'How the hell do I know!' I'd answered. She had not seemed to understand that I'd *needed* to go . . . to prove to her as well as myself that I wasn't a failure; that I *could* make a living as a painter.

I missed her terribly at first. I'd loved her with all the passionate ardour of any young man of twenty in love for the first time. Gradually, the coolness of her letters and her failure to plead with me to return, had their effect. I realized that the incessant rows and quarrelling must have got her down as much as they had me.

I glanced down at the child beside me – the child of our love – and I was suddenly afraid. I wished I were back in Spain where I had no ties – nothing that could threaten my freedom.

'Janie thinks my dad might be on the next plane!' the boy said, as much to himself as to me. 'I think he's probably lost. It's easy to get lost in an airport – there's so many passages.'

I asked him how old he was.

'I'm six. I'll be seven next year.'

I was touched by the way he drew himself up stiffly to gain another few inches.

'If I can't be a pilot, I'm going to be a foot-baller,' he announced. 'I want to go to a football match, but Mum says it's dangerous. Toby – he's my friend – often goes to them. His dad takes him.'

'Perhaps your dad will take you!'

He shook his head.

'I don't expect he will. Mum says he's coming on business and probably won't stay long. He's too

26

busy painting things all over the world. I'd like to go all over the world but Mum says artists want to be on their own.'

So Patti hadn't told him that our separation was to be final; that we were shortly to become one of the 'one-in-three statistics' for divorce. Maybe it was one-in-two for couples who'd married when they were little more than children themselves.

I could see the air hostess was now chatting on the phone. One part of me wished she would hurry up and reclaim the boy; another less welcome part needed more time. Remembering my surprise that my son had not recognized me, I said, 'What's your dad look like then?'

Paul seemed unsurprised by my curiosity.

'I'll show you,' he said, pulling a dog-eared photograph out of the pocket of his anorak. It was an old one – taken the summer before I went to Spain. I looked at it horrified, seeing a rather lean, excessively untidy drop-out with over-long hair and a shaggy beard. It had been my wanting-to-look-like-Gauguin phase, I recalled. What a ridiculous, stupid young poseur I'd been!

Some of my inner feeling of repulsion must have shown in my expression. Paul was frowning. To reassure him, I said quickly, 'You don't look a bit like him!'

'Mum says I used to. She says I look more like her now, but I'm growing up to behave just like my dad. Granny says "Heaven forbid!" I don't think Granny liked my dad very much. She often says nasty things about him. Mum gets cross when she does.'

Good for Patti! Granny's attitude was not news, however. Patti's mother had never liked me. Looking back, I could see why. Penniless, jobless, I must have seemed a very bad choice of husband for her only daughter; and my irresponsibility in landing her with a baby even before we were married was the last straw. In those days, her antagonism had spurred us both on to embark on a marriage for which we were undoubtedly far too young. Patti had been only just eighteen and was so beautiful, she could have taken her pick from a dozen other boyfriends. Poor Granny! At least she had been proved right in her predictions of disaster, and she must have been delighted when she finally got Patti all to herself again. Perhaps it was she who had talked Patti into asking for a divorce. I wondered now if it really was what Patti herself wanted; if, in fact, it was what I wanted.

'Why didn't your mother come to meet your dad?' I asked Paul.

'She's looking after Geraldine – my sister,' he explained. 'It's boring having a sister. She always wants to play with my toys.'

My heart was hammering.

'How old is she?'

'Nearly three.'

I was shattered. The child must have been conceived before I went away. Not only did I have a son who did not know me, but I had a daughter of whom I was totally ignorant. Why hadn't Patti told me? Geraldine – feminine of Gerald, my name. I felt very angry. Patti had had no right to keep such a thing from me. If I had known, I would not have left her. Was that the reason she had remained silent? If I had stayed, she would have known that the news of another baby on the way would keep me tied – not my love for her. She wouldn't have wanted that . . .

'You all right, Paul?'

The air hostess had returned and was smiling at me in a way that was a definite come-on; but I was no longer in the mood to appreciate her attributes.

'I'm OK. We're talking!' Paul replied seriously.

The girl gave me a quick look, decided I was harmless, and announced that she was going to make another call.

'The plane will be in soon,' she said as she went back to the telephones.

'Will you be very disappointed if your father isn't on it?' I asked.

It was a silly question and I should not have been miffed by the answer.

'I don't suppose it'll make much difference really.'

How could it! They were well accustomed to being without me.

'Perhaps your mother . . . !'

'I don't think so. She was going to buy a new dress but Granny said it was a waste of money, seeing as how my dad probably wouldn't stay long, so Mum bought a new winter coat for Geraldine and this anorak for me instead. Granny said it was a sensible thing to do and she was glad Mum had come to her senses at last.'

The boy was frowning.

'I suppose Granny's right – but when Mum got Dad's letter saying which plane he'd be on, she bought a whole lot of magazines and found a dress she really, really wanted. It was a sort of white lacy thing with beads all over it. I didn't think it was anything special but she said it would make her look like a princess. I think stories about princes and princesses are stupid. I like books about space, but Mum really did want it – until Granny put her off. I don't like it when she looks sort of sad.'

I knew exactly what he meant. I'd seen that lost, helpless look on Patti's face so often after one of our blazing rows and I'd been regretting my vile temper but was too proud to apologize. It had torn me to pieces – and so I'd run away.

'What do you want most in the world?' I asked my son. I knew it wouldn't be me!

'To go to a football match!' he said without hesitation.

'And Geraldine?'

'Oh, she likes eating. She's very greedy, and ever so fat. She's . . . '

He broke off as his escort beckoned to him. Another plane-load of passengers were pouring through the Customs doors. 'I've got to go now,' he said, standing up.

I stood up too, and held out my hand. He looked pleased and shook it hard, delighted with the man-to-man relationship I was implying.

'I hope we meet again,' he said politely. I could see my ma-in-law's training – Manners Maketh Man! Perhaps after all she was right to be so adamant. Perhaps she had always been right . . .

'I'm sure we will,' I said, and I, too, walked away to make enquiries as to the time of the next train to town.

*

I was furious when Gerry telephoned to say he'd been delayed and wouldn't be arriving until the following day. It didn't seem to bother him when I told him Paul had been to the airport and hung around for hours waiting to meet him. I suppose I shouldn't have been surprised. He'd never really loved his son – or me. Mum's quite right. He's never been anything but irresponsible, inconsiderate and utterly selfish. As Mum said, what else could one expect of an artist?

When I stopped feeling angry, I realized I was disappointed. There was a tiny part of me which had gone on nurturing the childish, romantic notion that one day Gerry would come back to us; that despite all the rows and the way he walked out on us, Gerry did love me; that our ill-fated marriage might, like some fairy story, still end 'happily ever after'. After all, I used to comfort myself when I was in one of those maudlin moods, he had never asked me to divorce *him* despite our long separation. I was the one who wanted the divorce, so that I could marry Tim.

I'd long since got over the feeling of utter desolation and despair which had devastated me when he first announced he was going off to Spain to paint. I'd hated him then for hurting me so much. I still don't think he could have walked out on us if he'd really loved us; but I've come to terms with it. I've realized that truly creative people need a certain amount of freedom in order to create. I always knew his career was vitally important to him and I understand now that he felt he had to prove himself to me; to Mum; to himself. To give him his due, he has done so. The exhibition in London is recognition of the fact that he really does have

31

talent. According to his last letter, he is only going to be in England for a few weeks and then he is off to Italy. As for me – I've already decided to marry Tim.

Tim is everything Gerry is not. He is in banking and commutes every day to the City. His life is planned, orderly. Because he is exceptionally good looking, erudite and a first-class tennis player, he is the most popular bachelor in our neighbourhood, and I was immensely flattered when he chose to spend his spare time with me, rather than with the unmarried girls who chased him.

At first, this salve to my pride was the only reason I went out with Tim; but gradually, I began to like him for other reasons. For one, he is sweet with the children. Geraldine, in particular, adores him. He does not get on quite so well with Paul, mainly because their interests differ. Paul is so like Gerry at times – a dreamer with no sense of time or accuracy; and when things don't go the way he wants, he can erupt in violent tempers which always remind me of his father. I often wonder how Gerry would react to Paul now. He was a difficult baby and Gerry had no patience with him. Tim's patience is inexhaustible, and I am grateful for it.

Not unnaturally, seeing how young I was at the time I'd met Gerry, I was a virgin when I married him. Looking back, I can see that sex had played an enormously important role in our lives. With Gerry, the outside world had no importance for us when we made love, so when he left me, I missed him physically in a way that it's hard to describe. By the time I met Tim, I was so starved of love,

I really enjoyed it the first time he kissed me. I think Tim realized I'd have let him make love to me but, of course, he was much too nice to take advantage, as he put it. He kept his passion under control whereas Gerry and I . . .

I always tried not to harp on such memories. However, it was not so easy to stop myself imagining who might be sharing Gerry's bed in Spain. Everyone knew that Mediterranean women were very hot-blooded and I hated to think how much better they were than I at love making. There had only ever been Gerry in my life, but I never pretended to myself that he, of all people, would remain celibate! I suppose it was nothing more than feminine jealousy and until I met Tim, I'd always comforted myself with the thought that whoever else he fancied, Gerry would certainly not want to get married again. He needed to be free.

Now, as a taxi drew up at the door of the cottage and seconds later, the doorbell rang, my overriding emotion was one of acute nervousness. Determined as I was to conduct this meeting with a cool, impersonal sophistication, I drew a deep breath. I reminded myself firmly that I was no longer a child.

'Hullo, Patti! Hope you don't mind, I caught the two-thirty so I'm a bit early.'

The eyes, the voice, the face were the same; but I could hardly recognize him. He was wearing a well-cut suit; his hair was short – not too short – but nicely styled. Surely Gerry, of all people, had not been to a barber! In the old days, when his hair had got too long, he'd always made me trim it with the kitchen scissors!

33

I was suddenly conscious of the fact that I was wearing grubby jeans; that I had not, after all, done my own hair – in short, that I must look a mess. Hurriedly, I closed the front door and led the way into the sitting-room.

Unlike me, the room was tidy – too tidy really for comfort; but Mother *would* go round plumping up cushions and picking up the children's toys from the floor the moment we left the room. I was conscious of Gerry staring – not at the room, but at me. I wished he wouldn't. I found my voice – or at least a voice.

'Do sit down!' And when he did so, 'It's been a long time, hasn't it?'

The banality of the remark appalled me. Surely I could do better than that?

Gerry had been carrying a large parcel which he now put down on the floor.

'What's in there?' I heard myself asking. As if it was any of my business.

He smiled. I felt my heart lurch and then harden. I had no intention of falling victim to his charm a second time.

'A dress for a princess to wear at the ball tonight!'

I hadn't the slightest idea what he was talking about. I tried again.

'The children will be back soon. Mother has taken them for a walk!'

'Children?'

I turned quickly away from those dark, questioning eyes. For a moment, I'd forgotten he didn't know about Geraldine . . .

I told him the facts as briefly as I could. Oddly, he didn't seem in the least surprised – or angry

34

with me – for keeping him in ignorance of the birth of his own child.

'Why didn't you tell me at the time, Patti?'

Now I was angry – angry enough to drop my guard.

'Because it wouldn't have made any difference to our relationship. You wanted to leave me and you did. If you'd stayed, it would have been as a duty . . .'

'Your mother would have said so. I . . .'

Paul came into the room and he broke off. Paul was staring at Gerry, an odd look on his face. I supposed it did feel a bit strange coming face to face with a father he hadn't seen for three years.

'Hi, Paul!'

They shook hands like two adults.

'I've something for you!' Gerry said, but he did not reach for the parcel. He took an envelope out of his breast pocket. Mum came in with Geraldine as Paul gave a whoop of delight.

'Wow! Thanks! Great! Thanks a lot!'

Not money, surely, I thought, feeling as if I were walking on quicksand.

'Look, Mum – tickets for the Cup Final. Wow!'

Gerry stood up to greet my mother and offer her his chair. This show of good manners rendered her speechless. He was managing to surprise us all.

'Would Geraldine like one of these lollipops?'

Of course she would. She grabbed it, beaming. Mother found her voice.

'You'll spoil the child's tea, Gerry!' She bent down and tried to remove it from Geraldine's stubborn grasp. Geraldine won.

Gerry looked over Mother's head at me – and winked! It was that selfsame conspiratorial wink he used to give me when Mother turned up at our studio flat at inappropriate moments and said, 'I trust I'm not interrupting you!' Suddenly, I wanted to laugh. Instead, I hurried out of the room mumbling about getting some tea.

When I came back with the tea trolley, Gerry was looking like a thunderstorm. Paul was sitting quietly by his side. Geraldine was the only one unperturbed, sitting on the floor eating the forbidden lollipop.

'Gerald's manners don't seem to have improved with the years!' Mum said, her voice furious.

'I only told your mother that your future, my future and the children's were a matter I preferred to discuss with you, Patti, and not with her.'

'I was simply telling Gerald that you and Tim . . .'

'You'd no right to do so!' I interrupted. I was furious. I'd wanted to tell Gerry about Tim in my own way in my own good time. 'Anyway,' I added bitingly, 'seeing that you've brought up the subject, perhaps you would remove the children as soon as we have had tea, Mum. This is hardly a matter for them.'

I should have sent them away then and there. As it was, tea was a ghastly ritual. Neither Gerry nor I ate anything. Even Paul, who adores chocolate cake, only ate a bun and a biscuit. Geraldine, of course, ploughed through everything. Every once in a while, she turned and smiled sweetly – in fact coyly – at Gerry.

'Flirt!' he told her. He was obviously frightfully taken with the child. At that moment, I was not. I

36

was feeling bitter. It was so easy to be interested in your children and to find them delightful when you only saw them for a few hours once every three years!

Finally Mum departed with the children without addressing a word to Gerry.

He broke the silence.

'You'd better tell me about this chap your mother says you intend to marry!' he said in a stilted sort of voice. 'It would appear that this time, you have picked someone "eminently suitable".' He mimicked Mum's voice, his tone heavily sarcastic.

'Yes, he is! And . . . ' I added, wanting to hurt Gerry, ' . . . he's wonderful with the children. He wants me to tell you that he'd be more than happy to adopt them — if that's OK with you. He'll give them both a decent education and . . . '

Gerry's voice was ominously quiet. I remembered how this nearly always preceded a violent outburst of temper.

'You can tell him to mind his own damn business. I'm quite prepared to give you a divorce, if that's what you want, but he can keep his hands off my kids. I'll pay for their education — and anything else they need! Geraldine *is* my child, I take it? I presume you have named her after me?'

It was I who lost control. I swore at him; told him he had no right to insult me after all he'd done to ruin my life.

'You know damn well she's yours!' I said. 'I didn't even know of Tim's existence until we came to live down here, and even if I had, I've never slept with him!'

37

A strange look came over Gerry's face.

'Haven't you?' he said. 'Why ever not?'

'That's my business, not yours!' I shouted.

'Fair enough!' Gerry said. 'I apologize! Now about this divorce – it shouldn't be difficult seeing that we've lived apart all this time; or you could say I'd deserted you if you wanted.'

'I doubt it!' I replied, my anger cooling and my depression returning. 'Not with you sending us more than enough to live on.'

Gerry shrugged.

'Look, it's something we ought to be able to thrash out in a civilized manner. After all, we're both adults now; but frankly, I find it difficult with your mother and the kids next door. How about a meal in town – a sort of farewell dinner before I shoot off abroad again? Remember that little Italian restaurant we always used to go to on special occasions – near South Ken underground? I suppose it's still going strong?'

I nodded.

'It was open when I passed it a few weeks ago on my way to the studio.'

'You mean, you've still got the flat?' Gerry sounded astonished.

'There was no room here to store your canvasses!' I said defensively. 'Besides, it's only a peppercorn rent. It seemed the best place to keep them.'

Gerry nodded.

'I'll get the canvasses moved before I go,' he said. 'I hope the damp hasn't ruined them.'

'Oh, no!' I said quickly – too quickly. 'I've been up there once or twice to check on the place.' And to shed a few tears when one of my maudlin moods

38

got the better of me, I thought. I'd been so happy there – at any rate, in those early days.

'Then you can sell the lease – what's left of it!' Gerry said. 'Now how about that meal? Tonight?'

'No, it's . . . I always meet Tim on a Thursday. Anyway, I'm not sure . . . '

'Never on a Sunday?' Gerry laughed. 'What if you're not in the mood on a Thursday?'

'Don't be silly!' I said. I knew what he meant but I added defiantly, 'I'm always in the mood, Gerry. I enjoy being with Tim – and it's a break for me . . . from the kids!'

'OK! Tomorrow, then. Eight o'clock? You have a car, don't you?'

'Yes, of course!' I answered testily. 'How else could I get Paul to school or Geraldine to Mums and Tods. You just don't realize how . . . '

'What on earth is Mums and Tods?' Gerry broke in. I don't know why, but his ignorance at that moment made me laugh. He looked so bewildered. Then I felt angry again.

'I'm not sure if I can make it,' I prevaricated. 'I'll ring you, Gerry. Give me the number where you are staying. But don't expect me. Tim likes to take me swimming on Fridays and . . . anyway, I can't see that it's really necessary. We can write to each other about the divorce.'

Gerry seemed not to have heard the last part of my sentence.

'Still not on Sundays, then?' he said with a wicked smile. This time, I did not think it funny. He was obviously trying to make Tim sound utterly boring. But before I had a chance to eulogize about Tim's Tennis and Squash Club and the marvellous new indoor pool they'd just opened, Gerry was on the telephone to the local taxi service. Mum came back in to the room, and five minutes later, he was gone.

'You'd be very stupid going all the way up to London – and at night, too,' Mum said when I told her nothing had, as yet, been resolved but that I might be meeting Gerry in London tomorrow. 'You'll only let that man charm you into an agreement that's entirely to his benefit. He always could twist you round his little finger!'

'It's only twenty miles, Mum,' I said, deliberately ignoring her remark about Gerry. I felt profoundly irritated by the knowledge that she was absolutely right. Moreover, in my heart of hearts, I knew that whatever I might have said to Gerry, I wanted to go out to dinner with him – even if it was a farewell dinner. As soon as I opened the package mum started asking questions about the dress. I knew now what Gerry had meant when he'd bought it – he'd meant to ask me out and somehow he'd known that I'd badly wanted something new and really stunning to wear. But how . . . ?

I don't know if I have ever been so angry as I was later that evening when I found out. As I tucked Paul up for the night, he told me about Gerry being at the airport and wanted me to explain why his father had not identified himself but had waited until today. Whatever convoluted scheme had prompted Gerry's deception, I didn't know. What I did know was that yet again, he had made me suffer for his own nefarious purpose – and I *had* suffered when Janie had brought Paul back from Gatwick and told me Gerry had not turned up. I'd washed and blow-dried my hair; put on a decent dress and . . . well, I'd been terribly disappointed and, although I was only now prepared to admit it, worried in case Gerry had decided against coming back to England at all. Of course, he'd telephoned to say he'd be down that afternoon, but by then I'd had a sleepless night and Mum on and on at me saying how utterly typical this was of Gerry until I thought I'd scream.

Tim was wonderfully sympathetic and understanding when I went out to dinner with him that night.

'Of course you must go up to town and meet him if that's what you want, my dearest, but don't you think your mother may be right? Your ex does sound a bit unreliable, to put it mildly.'

'He isn't my ex yet!' I said nastily, but even then, Tim was patient with me.

'No, of course not. A slip of the tongue. But it really wasn't very fair of him to behave like that, was it? I mean, poor young Paul must have been terribly disappointed as well as confused. And while I think about it, Patti, trying to win the boy's approval with tickets for a football match, which we both agree can be a dangerous venue these days, is simple bribery. It'll only whet Paul's appetite and you'll be left with the problem of forbidding further occasions after Gerald has gone off to Italy.'

I'd forgotten Italy – a country I'd always longed to visit. We'd have gone to Florence on our honeymoon except we were broke and couldn't even afford a night in Bournemouth! Tim had offered to take me to Italy when we were married but somehow I'd lost the urge to go. It didn't stop

41

me resenting the fact that Gerry would be going there without me.

'I just don't understand what he's up to!' I said to Tim. 'I mean, it's not as if *he'd* asked *me* for the divorce, so why the softening up process?'

'Perhaps he took a fancy to young Paul at the airport and wants to make sure you'll let him have joint custody of the kids.'

'Access – but not custody!' I said emphatically.

'I can't see the courts refusing you sole control of the children seeing how Gerald has behaved in the past,' Tim said, taking my hand in his. He stroked the back of it gently. 'Moreover, I think I may impress them as being a responsible kind of chap, especially as I'm willing to adopt them; give them my name.'

It did not seem the right moment to tell Tim of Gerry's reaction to that idea.

'Tell you what, dearest,' Tim said as he told the waiter to bring us another bottle of wine, 'why not compromise? Tell Gerald you won't go up to town tomorrow but you'll go for lunch on Saturday. Then I could drive you up and, if you wanted, be in on the meeting – to give you a little support.'

I didn't think Gerry would welcome a three-some, but lunch instead of dinner was a good idea. Tim looked pleased when I said so.

'I can't bear to see you worried or unhappy,' he said, adding in a low husky voice, 'I love you so very much, dearest. Do you know, Patti, I've never seen you look so desirable.'

He was staring into my eyes with a look that was unmistakably passionate. He really was very, very attractive, most of all on the rare occasions

he had that hungry-for-sex look. I could feel my
body responding and for a moment, I would have
given everything for him to have swept me out
of the restaurant, driven me back to his flat and
made violent love to me. It was such a long time
since I'd felt young, silly, abandoned. I'd been a
celibate, frustrated, sensible mother, not a woman,
far too long.

I knew Tim would think I was mad to suggest
such a thing, but there was a second best.

'Tim, darling Tim!' I said. 'I honestly do believe we should . . . ' (It wasn't so easy to say as
I'd thought.) I tried again, 'Please, darling, afterwards, can we go back to your place for coffee?
We can't be alone here, can we?' I wasn't making
much sense, so I decided to call a spade a spade. 'I
want us to make love,' I said, my voice barely above
a whisper. 'I don't want to wait till we're married.
Nobody does these days and . . . and I need you.'

For several minutes, Tim said nothing, although
his grip on my hand tightened and he didn't let it
go when the waiter arrived and refilled our glasses.
Then he said:

'Do you really mean that, dearest? Are you sure
– quite sure?'

'Yes!' I said, my voice squeaking, and then in
something close to a shout: 'Yes, I do mean it.
Yes! Yes! Yes!'

I felt wonderfully elated in the train going back to
London. Not only was I 90 per cent certain Patti
would come up to meet me the following night,
but even more important, that she still loved me.
I'd been pretty shattered when her mother had

43

told me about the chap she was going to marry – Tim Something-or-other. It was the second shock of the day.

The first had been discovering that I'd fallen in love with Patti all over again. Perhaps, I thought now, I'd never really fallen out of love. I don't know if Patti realized what she had let slip when she said she had never slept with this new man in her life. No one knew better than I how passionate, sexy, she could be. Once she had got over her initial shyness, she was always as eager for love as I. Perhaps that was one of the reasons we quarrelled so much – we were both permanently exhausted! Of course, it had had to stop before Paul was born, and afterwards, when Patti was feeding him, she didn't feel like making love so often. Looking back, I suppose he was a pretty demanding baby, keeping her up at nights; and not much better as a toddler.

Ah, Mums and Tods, I thought as my train drew into Victoria Station, and I smiled. Thinking of mothers reminded me of Patti's. In those days my ma-in-law had spent most of her time when she visited us telling me how tired poor Patti looked and that I should be doing more of the chores. How angry that always made me! How could I get on with my painting if I had to stop to peel potatoes or wash up or take the dirty clothes down to the launderette? We'd not been able to afford a washing machine.

It was easy enough to see now, in retrospect, where everything had gone wrong. If only I could persuade Patti to give me another chance, I wouldn't make the same mistakes again.

As soon as I got back to my hotel, I booked a table for the following night at 'our' restaurant. Luigi, the owner, was still there . . . and he remembered us.

'So young-a, so in love-a!' he enthused. He was far too tactful to add that we were also 'so poor-a' that we could never afford more than one item on the menu!

My first warning of disaster was when Patti phoned my hotel next morning. She wanted to change the day. I told her I couldn't make Saturday – it was the first day of my exhibition and I'd have to be there. How about Saturday night, I asked, and because I was worried, I added waspishly, 'or is that your night to go jogging with the athletic boyfriend?'

Patti's voice was ice cold. 'I don't usually go out on a Saturday. It's Mum's evening for bridge.'

'Can't you ask her to change it? After all, I'm not in England for very long. Anyway, what's so important that you can't make it tonight?'

'I didn't say it was anything important – just that I wanted to make it Saturday! Forget it!' Patti said, and with that, she put the phone down.

I was angry, disappointed and too proud to ring her back and try to talk her round. I supposed that the wretched boyfriend had suggested something better to do than having dinner with me. By the time evening came, I wished I'd phoned back. I simply didn't know whether to go to Luigi's or not. Patti had not actually said she wouldn't come . . .

In the end, I took a taxi round to South Kensington but I didn't go inside. I didn't want to look a complete fool if she stood me up. Fortunately it wasn't raining, so I stayed near the entrance to Luigi's and waited.

I waited until half past eight. It was a half-hour in my life that I never want to repeat, for as the minutes ticked away, so did my hopes for the future. Patti would have come – if she still loved me. Somehow, I had talked myself into believing she did because it was what I wanted to believe. I knew now that I'd lost her – really lost her; and my kids, too. We were, after all, to become one of the 'one-in-three' divorce statistics.

The taxi driver thought I was quite mad when I gave him the address of my hotel and when we reached it, told him I wished to go back to South Kensington.

'You're paying, mate!' he said.

'I'm paying not only your fare but for a hell of a lot of past mistakes!' I said, which did nothing to alter his opinion of me.

I got out of the taxi at Luigi's and walked round to the mews where the studio was. For some reason, I still had the key on my key-ring. Of course, there was a reason but I did not want to remember that I'd planned to bring Patti here after our tête-à-tête dinner. As I fitted the key in the lock, I told myself another lie – that I had come here simply to collect my canvasses, not for a self-pitying wallow in nostalgic memories of days and nights that I knew now would never come again.

Climbing the stairs, I told myself sternly that grown men don't weep; that it was only in my head I could hear that incredibly sentimental song Patti used to love. *'These foolish things – remind me of you . . .* ' It sounded so real, as if that old record was still being played.

I opened the door. Patti was sitting on the floor, crying. Suddenly I knew that grown men did weep. I squatted down beside her and took her in my arms. She was the first to speak.

'I wasn't going to come . . . I thought . . . I wanted . . . I suppose . . . '

'Yes?' I said, my lips against her hair.

'I suppose now you're here, we ought . . . we should talk about . . . the divorce.'

'I suppose we should – but some other time!' I muttered. 'Right now, my darling, we've more urgent things to do. You don't think your mother will interrupt us, do you?'

'Probably!' Patti said, smiling through her tears.

I knew then that soon enough, we'd be off to Italy together and that we weren't going to be a divorce statistic after all.

May 2016

MessyMessy Fettes Row

Dear Aunt Cecelia,

It was great to see you looking well. In our imagination we had you looking totally listless & at least 20 years older.

Please keep it up as you are now head of the Morrison family.

Amir Amna & I hope to be over later in the summer so we can all look forward to going out to lunch - I remember a lovely time with you before at the Red Lion.

Here is the book I forgot to bring over last time. One of 2 of the stories have a sham ending. They reminded me of the Peoples Friend so I hope you enjoy them. Let me know what you think

Love, Ann

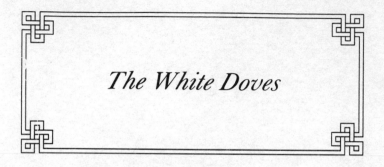

The White Doves

Connie stood on the Ponte Vecchio, her hand raised to her forehead to shade her eyes from the sun. Looking anxiously to her left and then to her right, she searched for a glimpse of Mrs Gilson's blue cotton dress. A moment or two ago, she had been entranced by the beauty of the old bridge and had stopped to stare down into the sparkling water of the River Arno flowing beneath her. In those few minutes she had somehow lost sight of her companions, and now suddenly she was overcome by panic. There were so many people milling past her; olive-skinned Italians and tourists like herself – foreigners who did not speak her language and who, according to Mrs Gilson's friend, Betty, might all too easily mug her and certainly would steal from her if she were not vigilant.

Feeling dizzy with the heat of the sun, Connie tried very hard to concentrate. Perhaps Mrs Gilson had returned to the square to look for her there. There had been tiled benches where she could sit down for a little while until the dizziness had passed.

A group of children ran past, jostling her and causing her to clutch her handbag more tightly. The mother smiled and said, ' *'giorno!*' but Connie did not feel up to returning the greeting. Although she had learned a few basic phrases, she knew she would be hopelessly lost if the woman started gabbling to her in Italian.

By the time Connie reached the square, she was aware of only two things – the heat of the sun and that she was lost. One of the cool tiled seats was unoccupied and she sat down quickly, her head swimming. As slowly it cleared, she was relieved to see that her hands were still gripping her handbag. At least she could take comfort from the fact that she had not lost it. It contained some Italian money and at the worst, if she could not find anyone she knew, she could take a taxi to her hotel. She regretted now that she had allowed Mrs Gilson to take possession of her passport – for safe keeping, the younger woman had said, not meaning to be hurtful, Connie was sure, but drawing attention to her forgetfulness. Now, if she were truly lost, she might need her passport. Provided she had this precious document, the courier had said, she could come to no harm.

The courier, a nice, friendly young woman called Maggie, seemed anxious that everyone should enjoy their holiday. Connie had tried to concentrate on the outpouring of information Maggie gave them every morning as the coach set off for its next destination, but she was not always able to concentrate. They had been travelling for three days in the big, air-conditioned coach but despite its comfort – it even had a toilet in the rear – Connie felt physically and mentally exhausted.

'The holiday will do you good, Mum!' her daughter had told her when she'd booked her on the coach trip to Italy. 'You must get fed up seeing only Fred and me and the kids. Change'll be good for you!'

Connie had not felt in need of a change. Now that she was getting so old, and even more forgetful, she was happiest in the familiar surroundings of home. Her teenage grandchildren were a bit noisy and Fred, bless him, did get a little cross with her when she lost the front door key or her pension book; but he was a good son-in-law, and as the social worker so often said, she, Connie, was fortunate to have a married daughter with a husband willing to let her live in their house. Otherwise she might have had to go into an old people's home.

If the truth were told, she had not wanted to go on the coach trip, but she had not become so stupid in her old age that she had failed to realize Noreen and Fred wanted to have their own holiday without her trailing along being a nuisance. They had gone to the Costa del Sol with the children, and with her out of the way, they'd been able to shut up the house.

'We certainly can't leave you here on your own, Mum!' Noreen had said when Connie suggested it as an alternative to her going away. 'It wouldn't be safe, and you'd never manage by yourself!'

Had she really become so old and incapable, Connie wondered? It was true she did have spells of forgetfulness – even forgetting her own name. She had had one of these spells in Marks & Spencer's and the store detective had found her wandering in the men's department and taken her to the rest room for a cup of tea. After he had found her pension book, he had rung directory enquiries and then telephoned Noreen to come and collect her in the car.

53

The coach trip, Noreen said, was the perfect solution to the problem of their summer holiday. It was for a party of elderly people like Connie; she would soon make friends; the courier would take care of her and Fred would pay all her expenses. Connie had felt unable to refuse.

How many days ago was it since Noreen had put her on the coach at Victoria? Three . . . no four! There'd been the sea crossing from Dover to Calais and then the drive to Peronne in France for the night. She had not slept very well although the hotel was clean and comfortable, but she'd been told to share a bedroom with Mrs Gilson who had wanted to talk. Mrs Gilson – although Connie was sure she meant well – was very annoyed with the courier because despite her pleas she had not been allowed to share a room with the two friends with whom she was travelling.

It was the same on the coach the next day. The seats were in pairs and Mrs Gilson had been put beside Connie and spent the long journey down the French motorway telling her about all the foreign places she had visited. Although Connie had been suitably impressed, she had been unable to take a quick nap and perhaps get rid of the nagging little headache which two aspirins had not dispersed.

Aware once more that she was lost and must not allow her mind to wander, Connie's eyes again searched the crowds in the sunlit square for a glimpse of Mrs Gilson's blue dress – the one she had bought especially for travelling, she'd pointed out, because it didn't crease. There was still no sign of her, and nor could Connie see any of the other

54

ladies on the coach trip. The courier had left them in the centre of Florence to do some shopping and see the sights, and had suggested that Mrs Gilson and her two friends kept an eye on Connie. They had not looked too pleased about it, preferring no doubt to be on their own, but never for one minute did it cross Connie's mind that they might have 'lost' her on purpose. Mrs Gilson, she reassured herself now, was a very experienced traveller and would come and find her.

This was their second day in Florence. Connie had been anxious to buy some little souvenirs for Noreen and Fred and the children, but Mrs Gilson insisted they must see the big cathedral and then the Ponte Vecchio before they shopped.

Two young girls in the briefest of shorts and sleeveless T-shirts sat down on the bench beside Connie, giggling and chattering in a foreign language. They eyed the old lady curiously. One established that she was English, but being Norwegian, could only manage a few faltering words. Neither of the girls could tell Connie where the coach that was to take her back to the hotel might be parked, or indeed, where the Hotel Florence Nord might be. The only information she gleaned from them was the worrying fact that it was nearly six o'clock. Connie had forgotten to put on her wrist watch after breakfast and had had no idea it was so late.

Perhaps, she thought as the girls moved away, she should try and find a policeman. This was what Noreen said she should do in England if she lost herself again. But would an Italian policeman speak English?

'One really shouldn't travel to a country if you can't speak a bit of the language!' Mrs Gilson had remarked when she'd discovered Connie's ignorance on their arrival in France. 'Never mind, I'm quite fluent so I'll do the necessary for you!'

But where was Mrs Gilson? On several occasions during the past four days, Connie had reproached herself for wishing Mrs Gilson, with her loud, bossy voice, a good many miles away! Now she would have given all her travellers cheques to see her buxom form approaching.

'It was that girl, Maggie's, duty to look after her, not mine!' Mrs Gilson said to her travelling companions. 'I didn't come on holiday to be saddled with a senile old woman. Trust her to get lost and ruin our afternoon!'

'She must be gone seventy!' Betty said sympathetically.

'Seventy-eight!' Mrs Gilson announced as they retraced their steps towards the cathedral. 'It's in her passport. Looks it, too!'

She straightened her back and allowed the new corset bra to show her bust to its best advantage. At fifty-five, she still had a figure worthy of admiration. To the envy of her friends, she had been enjoying a delightful verbal flirtation with their Italian coach driver – a young man with astonishingly white teeth and a wicked gleam in his large dark eyes. Only one of the ladies on the coach trip had a husband travelling with her. The others, like herself, were widows or spinsters.

'Here we are, in one of the most romantic cities in the world, and because of that stupid old woman, we're wasting our time looking for her!' she elaborated, pretending to disregard the suggestion of a middle-aged Italian to join him for a drink of coffee.

'Ignore him!' she told her envious companions. 'You can't trust these foreigners – they're all sex mad!'

'It's the heat, I dare say,' said Betty, wondering what it would be like to have a wildly passionate holiday romance with an Italian lover. Not that there was much hope for her – she had always been a Plain Jane; but Mrs Gilson was a fine looking woman – and so confident!

'It's quite hopeless trying to find the poor old dear in these crowds!' she was saying. 'We'll just have to hope she finds her way back to the coach. Maggie will know what to do if she doesn't turn up.'

At seven o'clock, when the coach was due to leave, the courier made them wait a further half-hour in the hope that Connie would appear. When she failed to do so, Maggie went to the police station to report her missing.

Finally, the coach left and the speculation as to what might have happened to Connie continued all the way back to the Hotel Florence Nord and throughout supper. The suppositions became wilder and by bedtime everyone agreed with Mrs Gilson that the poor old dear was probably lying in a back street with her throat cut and her travellers cheques and wedding ring stolen.

As the shadows deepened, so did Connie's panic. She realized that the coach must have left by now and that there was no hope of Mrs Gilson or her

friends finding her. Summoning her last vestige
of will-power, Connie hailed a passing taxi.

'*Dove, Signora?*' the driver asked, concerned to
see this dishevelled elderly tourist on her own so
late in the afternoon.

Connie could no longer remember the name
of her hotel. Her mind was a complete blank.
The driver waited patiently until, moved by her
obvious distress, he asked gently, '*Inglese?* You
English lady?'

'Yes, yes, I'm English!' Connie said. 'You speak
English? I'm afraid I am lost. I can't remember . . .
Mrs Gilson has my passport . . . I came on a coach
and . . .'

Enrico, the young taxi-driver, was reminded
suddenly of his late grandmother whose inco-
herent babblings and occasional sorties into the
village in her night clothes had been accepted by
the family as inevitable. After all, she had been
over eighty!

'*Non importante!* We go *il Posto di Polizia!*'

'Yes, yes please!' Connie said, allowing herself to
be helped into the taxi and sinking back gratefully
into the shabby interior which smelt of garlic and
strong tobacco.

To keep up his passenger's morale, Enrico sang
as he wound his way through the streets. Connie
recognized 'La Paloma' and felt better. Mrs Gilson,
had she been here, would have warned her that the
young man would undoubtedly try to take advantage of the situation and probably demand double
the correct fare; but, Connie decided, she wouldn't
mind if he did so. It would be worth it just to be in
the safe hands of the police.

The following half-hour was one of confusion. It seemed that a birthday party was in progress at the police station. There was a great deal of noise as everyone talked at once, and a great deal of wine was being drunk. The helpful Enrico seated Connie on a bench whilst he made her problems known to the man in charge. He was grinning when he returned.

'They say we stay . . . drinka the wine . . . have gooda time!' he said. 'You no stay . . . you very tired. *Domani* . . . tomorrow . . . *polizia* telephona hotella, *si*!'

Connie felt the panic returning. She clutched her handbag nervously.

'But tonight? Where will I go tonight?'

Enrico beamed.

'You coma *mi casa* . . . Papa, Mama, very pleasa. Papa speka good *Inglese* – He *Inghilterra* in war.'

He nodded towards the party and grinned.

'Sleepa here in *Posto* no gooda – *molto musica, molto vino! Celebrazione, si?*'

It was on the tip of Connie's tongue to suggest that Enrico might drive her to a hotel, but she was far from sure if she had sufficient money to pay, or indeed how to go about booking a room, or even selecting a suitable hotel. She was feeling very faint and there seemed no alternative but to trust her friendly taxi-driver. Discounting Mrs Gilson's warnings, she had no reason to mistrust foreigners; moreover, she thought, if Enrico had intended to rob or harm her, he had already had ample opportunity to do both!

Half an hour later, Connie found herself sitting in an armchair in an impeccably clean, whitewashed room whilst Maria, Enrico's mother, bathed her forehead and gave her a long cool drink made from freshly squeezed lemons. Paulo, the father, seated opposite her, was explaining everything to her in excellent English. He, it transpired, had been a prisoner-of-war and worked on a farm in Yorkshire.

'English family very good to me,' he said. 'We not enemies – we great friends. At Christmas we send card and one day I go back to England to see family. Maria and I very happy to have the chance to help English lady in distress. You no need to worry – we take care of you now.'

The whole family fussed over her – but not in a disturbing way. Connie began to relax and soon she was sitting up and telling them about her own family and the coach trip and how she had become lost.

A meal was produced by Maria and they were joined by Enrico's grandfather – an old man who must be at least her age, Connie thought, although he certainly did not behave like it. He was, she realized, treating her as if she were a young girl, flirting with her, despite the fact that he spoke no English.

'*Il nonno* say you have most beautiful hands – lika the white birds!' Enrico said laughing.

'*Le colombe!*' explained Paulo who was also laughing. 'In England, you call them doves. He say he is much in love. You stay here in Italy and he marry you!'

'Goodness gracious!' Connie said, feeling her cheeks colour. 'Please tell your grandfather I am seventy-eight years old!'

There was another spate of conversation between the entire family which Connie did not understand. Then Paulo translated for her.

'My father say in Italy no one too old to fall in love. He tell Enrico to sing song for you – how do you say, *fare una serenata*?'

Enrico reappeared with a guitar and at his grandfather's instruction, he played and sang 'La Paloma'. Soon, they were all singing, Connie humming the words when she recognized the refrains.

Halfway through the evening, Connie suddenly remembered the name of her hotel. At once, Enrico offered to drive her there despite the fact that it was getting quite late. The grandfather broke into a flood of words which Paulo, smiling, repeated in English.

'He say his heart break if the beautiful English lady depart one minute before is necessary!'

Paulo and Maria added their persuasions and Enrico assured her he would guarantee she was reunited with her friends before the coach left in the morning.

Connie decided to stay.

Outside the house, night had fallen and from the hill-top looking down towards the city, Florence was ablaze with lights. Below, like toys, the headlights of the cars speeding along the Autostrada del Sole seemed very far away.

Standing in the doorway as Paulo pointed out the sights, Connie was suddenly conscious of the fact that tomorrow the air-conditioned coach would be heading southwards down that very motorway to their next overnight stop in Rome. She wondered why – now that she knew she was no longer lost – she felt no great anxiety to be on it.

When finally she settled down to sleep in a tall brass bed opposite which hung a brightly painted picture of the Madonna and Child, Connie reflected guiltily that in many ways, she would greatly have preferred to spend all her holiday here in this simple little house with its warm-hearted family. Mrs Gilson had extolled the beauties of Rome, the Bay of Naples, the Isle of Capri, as indeed had Noreen and Fred. Noreen had said very firmly that you were never too old to be educated, to enjoy new experiences; but somehow all the travelling and sightseeing had been a little exhausting. Here in this house was peace. *Le colombe*, the white dove of peace . . . *'such pretty white hands . . .' 'you are never too old for love . . .'*

Connie was smiling as she drifted into sleep.

'You certainly cut it fine, Constance!' Maggie said reproachfully as the coach finally drew away from the Hotel Florence Nord and headed slowly through the traffic towards the motorway. 'At least we can be thankful you're safe!'

Mrs Gilson, who for once had actually fought to sit next to Connie, said importantly, 'Don't worry – we'll keep a closer eye on her in future. Now Connie, I want to hear all about it. What *did* happen to you?'

Throughout the previous evening, the entire coach party had speculated as to Connie's fate. Had she been murdered? Robbed? Or worse still, raped? Had she fallen into the River Arno? Been kidnapped? Was she dead in some dark, seedy alley? Everyone had agreed that Connie's daughter had had no right to let her elderly mother take such a trip; that undoubtedly Connie was suffering the onset of senile dementia; and that although she could not help it, poor old thing, her being there had spoiled – just a little – their own enjoyment of their holiday.

'I'm sorry you were all worried!' Connie replied to Mrs Gilson's question. 'I spent the night with an Italian family. They were very kind.'

She was about to explain about the birthday party at the police station but caught herself up at the last minute, certain that neither Mrs Gilson nor her friends would believe such a thing were possible. Mrs Gilson was asking more questions. Who were these Italians who had befriended her? Had they overcharged her? Hadn't she been afraid to trust herself to a foreign taxi-driver? What if he had driven her down a dark alley and robbed her?

Connie stopped listening. From her window seat, she could see far up on the hill the tiny white house which had been her haven. The old grandfather had said he would sit outside all day until their coach went past and that he would wave to her. She couldn't see him at such a distance but she did not doubt he was there. Paulo and Maria, too, had promised to wave.

'I think she's dropped off!' Mrs Gilson whispered over her shoulder to her friend. 'It's really been too much for her at her age! I don't expect we'll have her with us next year!'

No, thought Connie, I won't be with you!

Safely tucked away in her handbag was a piece of paper which was far more important to her than her travellers cheques or her passport.

'You take aeroplane – not so tiring!' Paulo had said. 'Enrico will meet you at the *aeroporto*. You rest in the sunshine, talk to the old man. We give you good holiday. Maria say too many men in this house; is good to have English lady. Enrico say he learn to speak good English accent iffa you our guest. No, you notta pay us nothing. I owe many kind things from English family in war. You comma stay for holiday in my house, I feel happy.'

'You feeling all right, Constance?' Maggie asked.

'Oh, yes, thank you, my dear!' Connie answered. Who would not feel all right knowing that they were really wanted? Knowing that even when you were seventy-eight, someone thought your hands were like little white doves?

The Angel and the Witch

or

Miss Tansley's Easter Play

Lillian Tansley eased herself further back on the hard wooden bench and some of the tension of the past week went out of her. The dress rehearsal had gone without too many hitches. If only the young cast could reach this standard again in tomorrow's performance the Easter play might not be the awful flop she had foreseen at earlier rehearsals. At least the children were enthusiastic now and the mums had done really well with their costumes.

The idea of having this end of term play had evolved one morning when she had questioned her primary class of thirty-six children.

'It will be Easter Sunday soon. Now what does this special day mean to you?' she had enquired.

'Chocolate eggs!'

'Bunnies!' That had come from Isobel, the youngest child in her class.

'And what else?' she had prompted.

'Holidays!'

They were all staring at her with blank faces. It had shocked Lillian to realize that these young children knew nothing of the real meaning of Easter. In the staff-room, she had voiced her dismay to the headmaster.

'I know it's awful, Lillian, but there's not much we can do about it, other than tell them the story and hope they'll remember.'

'I'll think of something to make them remember!' Lillian had declared.

That night, she sat up until two in the morning writing a simple little play, putting the beautiful words of St Luke into language the children would understand. Next day, she had read the story to them and when she had finished, her eyes, as always, went to Pete Brown. Although by no means the oldest in the form, Pete was the undisputed leader. By sheer strength of character, his will prevailed.

'Us act a *religious* play!' He grinned disarmingly. 'Not likely!'

'I think it would be fun, Pete. We'd use real make-up and you'd all have costumes. As a matter of fact, I thought you might like to be the Angel who rolls the stone away from the Sepulchre?'

She surveyed his crew-cut speculatively. With the stubble covered, he wouldn't look too bad as an angel.

Pete succumbed to the bait.

Over this first hurdle, there was another. Pete wanted the story to end with the actual Resurrection.

'We could do it easy, Miss, with wires and fings. I seen it done last Christmas on telly in Peter Pan. 'Course, that's a wimpy story but the flying part's OK.'

'No!' said Lillian firmly. 'I'm sorry, Pete, but no!'

Pete had survived the disappointment and rapidly undertaken the jobs of stage manager and prompter, as well as the role of the Angel. He became the most enthusiastic member of the cast. He bullied the others into rehearsals, organized his friends to help write invitations and stayed

68

late to help Lillian splash paint on the card-
board scenery.

He drew the curtains across the stage now and
looked down at her from the platform with a question mark in his brown eyes.

'Well?' he asked.

'It's fine, just fine!' Lillian said.

A smile caught the corners of her mouth as
she watched Cynthia Muggeridge climb down
off the platform. Cynthia was the prettiest girl
in the class, with long fair hair and blue eyes
– the obvious choice for the role of the Virgin
Mary. But Cynthia, whilst possessing God's gift
of physical beauty, was not very bright and so shy
that at first, not even Pete had been able to prevail
upon her to accept such an important part in the
Easter play.

'Ooh, I couldn't! I just couldn't!' she had protested over and over again.

It was Cynthia's mum who had finally solved
the problem.

'She'll do it – if I say she can wear her ballet
dress, Miss Tansley. She's always on at me about
it.'

'Oh, no, Mrs Muggeridge. The folds of the
Virgin Mary's dress should hang loose and soft
. . . stiff net would never do . . .'

Cynthia, on the brink of achieving her heart's
desire, possessed the stubbornness of the stupid.
A compromise was reached. Now, although the
blue dress billowed out over the stiff ballet skirt
like a crinoline, hopefully the audience would be
lulled by the sight of Cynthia's serene, pretty face
and accept her in her role.

69

'Now, don't forget, children, you are to assemble here immediately after lunch tomorrow. We'll have less than half an hour to get all of you dressed and made up.'

Pete walked part of the way home with her. As usual, he was talkative.

'Going to be a smash hit, in'it, Miss!' he said confidently. 'Me and the gang never thought as how there'd be all them exciting fings in the Bible. I mean – take this play – it's got magic in it, and ghosts an' all.' Seeing Lillian's expression, he added: 'You know, Miss – the body disappearing – like something in "Starsky and Hutch". Then there's the bit about Jesus coming back as a ghost and keeping His promise to fly up to Heaven where no one couldn't torture Him no more and He could save people.'

Lillian smiled happily. Even if the play were a flop tomorrow, tough little Pete had some idea now what Easter was all about.

Pete's cheerful whistle dwindled as he walked the last part of the way home on his own. Truth to tell, he wasn't feeling so good. His face and even his neck hurt – sort of ached, he decided. He put a grubby hand up to the side of his cheek and winced. There was a definite swelling.

'What's up with you then?' his mum asked sharply as she gave him a quick, piercing once-over.

'It's me neck!' Pete said doubtfully.

Mrs Brown observed the swelling.

'Oh, lor'!' she gasped. 'You've got the mumps – that's what!'

70

Nearly every child in the village had gone down with it this past term but Pete, miraculously, had escaped – until now.

Pete was looking at her, horrified.

'It can't be!' he shouted. 'I'm the Angel wot rolls back the stone. There's a sort of green light on me so I look kind of ghostlike,' he added frantically. 'I've got to be there tomorrow, Mum. I just *got* to.'

'Angel or no, if it's the mumps, you can't go,' Mrs Brown said flatly. 'Now off to bed with you, me lad. I'll bring your tea up later when your dad gets home.'

'But I'm feeling OK, Mum . . .'

'Bed!' repeated Mrs Brown, and marched him upstairs. As soon as she had left his room, Pete leaned out of his window and shouted to his friend, Lee, who lived in the other half of their semi-detached.

'Cor!' Lee said when he heard of Pete's misfortune. 'Glad it's not me!'

'But I gotta be the Angel!' Pete protested desperately. 'Miss Tansley's counting on me – she said so. We gotta think of something.'

'We could try a miracle!' Lee suggested.

'What – you?' Pete said scornfully. 'Only holy people can do them. Think of something else!'

'Maybe we could cut the lump off – with your new penknife!' Lee said after a moment's thought. 'On telly last week . . .'

'Don't be daft!' Pete interrupted. His jaw ached and the swelling seemed to be getting larger by the minute. He was dangerously near to tears he could not possibly shed.

71

'Well, maybe you could ask the Witch – ask her to make a spell.'

Pete's eyes narrowed thoughtfully. Maybe it was not such a silly suggestion. The Witch lived in one of the farm cottages a mile out of the village. She'd materialized some months ago after old Mrs Penshurst had died. His mum – who'd heard someone say so in the surgery – said she was Mrs Penshurst's niece; but one of the big boys at school had actually seen the witch – not her face, mind, but her tiny, hunched-up body with hands like claws. Granted he'd seen no sign of a broomstick, but she'd been hobbling about with the aid of two sticks; *and* she had a black cat.

Cynthia's mum had told Pete's mum that the district nurse went to Rose Cottage twice a week to bath the newcomer because she couldn't manage to get in and out of the bath by herself, she being 'an invalid who had been very badly burned in a fire.' None of the children believed this story. They had decided that the grown-ups had invented it because Silly Cynthia had had nightmares about the witch ever since she'd heard the boys saying one was living in Rose Cottage.

Pete, Lee and two of their friends, had dared go down the lane to see the newcomer for themselves, but the witch had known they were spying and had stayed behind the front room curtains; so they'd only been able to certify the existence of the black cat. It had terrified the life out of them, coming unexpectedly through the privet hedge behind which they were hiding, carrying a dead bird in its mouth. The cat had shot indoors when it saw them, still carrying the corpse in its mouth. The older boys said the witch probably had to use birds for her spells now there weren't so many toads about – because of something called 'conversation'.

'You too scared to go and ask her?' Lee's voice broke in on Pete's thoughts, neatly crystallizing his fears. He *was* scared, but apart from not wanting to admit it to Lee, there was no other way he could think of getting rid of the mumps.

'Course I'm not! 'S a good idea. We'll go now, shall we?'

The collective noun did not escape Lee's notice.

'Me – go with you? Not likely!' he said.

'I'll give you my penknife. It's nearly new.'

Lee hesitated.

'And you can borrow my skateboard whenever you want.'

Lee scratched his head.

'OK!' he said at last.

'You can write out an invitation to the play for her while I'm getting me clo's on!' Pete announced.

'You mean you're going to ask the Witch to come and see the play?'

'Course I am! You don't s'pose she'd make me a spell for nuffink, do you? And Miss Tansley said everyone wants to go to the play and there's only room for the ones as have got invitations – and nobody else is gonna give her one.'

Lee shrugged. He was far from sure a witch would want to go to school or, indeed, if Miss Tansley would want a witch in the audience. Besides, Silly Cynthia would drop down dead with fright if she saw her. But he knew better than to argue with his friend once Pete had made up his

73

mind. He closed the window and went to search in his satchel for a clean piece of paper and his pen.

The clock struck five. Dorothy Amble stirred in her chair by the fire and shivered. Presently, she'd make herself a cup of tea and then, since there was nothing else to do, she'd spend another evening reading or watching television. But, crippled as she was, doing anything at all required an effort of will, and somehow of late, she seemed to be losing a little – no, a lot – of her willpower.

'No such word as can't!' the kindly but strict physiotherapist had said so many times when she'd been in hospital learning to walk again. She, Dorothy, had believed it then, but it wasn't so simple now that she no longer had the other patients, doctors and staff to bolster her morale. She'd thought that regaining her independence, however limited, was the most important thing in the world and had never doubted that she could manage when her aunt had died and left her this cottage in the country. It had taken her quite a while to persuade her specialist that she would be perfectly happy living on her own; that she didn't need a companion. It might have been different if she could have shared a home with one of her sisters, but they, like her brother and both her parents, had died in the fire that had left her a twisted, useless cripple.

After three months of living alone, with only the twice-weekly visits of the district nurse to look forward to, she was willing to admit that even the company of a stranger would be welcome. No one in the village had called to see her. Occasionally she

74

had glimpsed children in the lane and once in the garden, but they had been either too frightened or too shy to come closer. She did not blame them, for despite the innumerable operations the plastic surgeon had performed, the scarring had left her body and limbs horribly distorted.

She tried now to take comfort from the fact that soon it would be Easter. Until the accident, she had always gone with her family to church to rejoice in the hope and promise the service symbolized. She would like to go this Easter but she could never walk the distance. Moreover, her Faith had taken a hard knock and she knew herself deeply resentful of a God who had allowed her life to end at thirty. She had no hope of marriage now; no hope of bearing children. She did not have a family or friends or even neighbours to comfort her; lessen her loneliness.

It was all very well being given the promise of a life hereafter, she told herself, close to tears. But what about *this* life? It was this one which she must face tomorrow, the next day and the next. She was not sure if she could bear another long, meaningless day here in the cottage. Maybe she should sell it and buy a flat in a town where she might at least see other people passing by. Maybe she should never have allowed her love for the country and village life to overrule the more practical aspects that must face a handicapped person.

She was just easing herself out of her chair with the aid of her two crutches when she heard the knock on the door. She would have been less surprised to see Prince Charles than the two untidy small boys standing in the porch.

75

Pete thrust a grubby piece of paper towards her and quickly put his hand in his pocket before the Witch's claw could touch him.

'For you!' he said. He hoped his voice wasn't shaking, his knees certainly were. Now that he was actually face to face with the Witch, he was even more frightened than he had anticipated.

Lee was staring over the hunched shoulders of the little woman at her black cat stretched out in front of the fire. There was no sign of a cauldron.

'Oh, how kind, how very kind!' Dorothy said as she read the invitation. She blinked back the tears which had sprung to her eyes. 'Why, I can't think of anything I'd like better! Of course I'll come. I'd love to . . .'

Then she remembered the mile long walk and said shakily: 'That is, I would love to have gone but I can't walk to the village and I don't have a car.'

'Can't you fly?' Lee asked. Surely all witches had broomsticks even if they didn't have cars.

Pete was more matter of fact. Mistaking Dorothy's failure to grasp Lee's meaning, he assumed the invitation by itself was not a good enough offering to tempt the witch.

'My Dad'll take you in our van!' he improvised quickly. After all, if the spell worked, it would mean she was a proper witch and his dad would be only too pleased to be on the right side of her. He'd often told Pete: 'It's never a bad idea to be on the right side of them as can do you harm!'

The witch was looking happy again. She was positively beaming. In fact, she really didn't have a witch's face at all, Pete thought. She was quite

76

pretty – like Miss Tansley – and had a nice soft voice like his teacher's. It was probably one of her spells, he decided, to trick him and Lee into thinking she was ordinary; but it seemed a bit silly not to have changed her ugly, twisted body at the same time.

'Come in, children! Come in! I was just about to make a cup of tea. I'm afraid I haven't got any biscuits or cake but please do come in.'

Pete hesitated. There was no point in braving the interior of the cottage until he was sure the Witch could help him. He pointed to his face.

'Can you do anything about this?' he asked bluntly. 'Me mum won't let me go to school tomorrow if it stays like this – and I'm the Angel in the play.'

Dorothy reached up and touched, very gently, the swollen jaw.

'I'm afraid it might hurt a bit. Is it hurting now? Couldn't you wait till tomorrow and get your mum to take you to . . . '

'No, I can't wait!' Pete interrupted desperately. 'I don't care if it hurts. I just gotta get rid of it by morning else Mum'll never let me be the Angel wot rolls back the stone.'

Dorothy wasn't quite sure what the child meant, but he looked close to tears and the tooth was already very loose. It would only need a gentle tug, so perhaps his mum wouldn't mind her pulling it out although she could easily have done the job herself.

Lee, interested and apprehensive in equal parts, followed Pete into the cottage and watched as his friend was urged into a chair.

'Shut your eyes and count five,' said the Witch. 'Then I'll count five and it'll all be over.'

Shutting your eyes and counting five did not strike Lee as much of a spell. Nevertheless, Pete was counting. The Witch bent over him and Lee jumped nervously as Pete gave a muffled yelp.

'There!' said the Witch. 'That's all over. Just go into the bathroom – through that door over there – and spit out the blood. Then I'll give you a sweet to take away the taste.'

Five minutes later, as the boys walked home, Pete felt his swollen face and said in a small flat voice, 'You know what she did, don't you? She didn't do nuffink to the lump – just pretended she was going to and then took out a tooth. There's a hole in the back. I don't believe the lump will be gone by morning like she said.'

'Maybe she needed a tooth to make the spell work!' Lee suggested. ' 'S funny, isn't it, her asking us to tea next week and saying she'll make a ginger cake and all.'

'I don't believe she's a witch at all!' Pete muttered. He was once more on the verge of crying. Suppose in the morning the swelling hadn't gone down as she'd promised? Suppose the other side swelled up, too? His mum would be sure to check and then he'd never get to be in the play!

'It's damn, effing, bloody!' he said as they parted company to make their way to their respective homes. Lee knew that it wasn't the tooth Pete was referring to but his luck; and that he'd used the worst swear words he knew to describe a rotten old disease called mumps.

*

Dorothy Amble sat between Mrs Brown and the
vicar. The Easter play was almost over. As Lillian
had feared, there had been one or two hitches. The
elastic in Cynthia's pants had given way and they
had had to be removed on stage behind the figure
of Mary Magdalene in scene one. Then the Angel,
removing the stone in scene two, was bathed in a
furious red glare when Lee had switched on the
wrong spotlight. Pete was remarkably unaffected,
though at the time Lillian had held her breath,
expecting him to turn and bash his effects man in
the heat of the moment. Only after the play ended
did she understand Pete's restraint.

'That red light made it look just like Hell!' he
said with a grin. 'Smash hit, wasn't it, Miss!'

'Charming!' 'Delightful!' 'So sincere!' the parents
were commenting. The vicar nodded approvingly,
delighted with this excellent start in his new parish.

Only Dorothy Amble said nothing. There were
people all around her chair.

'You must forgive me for not having called on
you as yet,' the vicar was saying. 'But I'm new in
the parish, too, and I've been so busy, I haven't had
time to meet everyone. I do hope you will come
home and have some tea with me this afternoon,
and then I can run you back to your cottage in
my old Mini!'

'I hope the boys' invitation was neat and clean,'
said Lillian Tansley. 'I inspected all the others but
I don't think I saw yours!' How fortunate, she
thought, that she'd found an extra chair; and why
hadn't Pete or Lee told her they were going to
invite the newcomer? Before the children broke
up for the holidays, she must give them a talk about

disfigured and handicapped people and explain why it was unkind to stare.

Dorothy was aware of the stares, but these she had expected. The warmth of the adults around she had not.

'I'm your nearest neighbour!' Cynthia's mum was saying. 'I'd have called to see you only I've just had the twins and I've been that busy with them, and extra clothes to make seeing as how we were only expecting one!'

'Maybe I could help!' Dorothy offered hesitantly. 'I used to be a dressmaker before . . . before the accident, but I can still sew, though I am a bit slow.'

'Ooh, would you really, Miss Amble? I'd be ever so grateful. I've ever such a lot of material and . . . could I bring some round one morning?'

'Our Lee said you were going to make a ginger cake for when he and Pete go to tea with you next week. It's my husband's favourite, and if you could possibly let me have the recipe . . . He doesn't like shop-bought cakes, you see . . . '

'Did you say you was a *dressmaker*?' Pete couldn't keep the question back any longer. 'I mean . . . always? Not nothing else, like a . . . ?'

His mum trod firmly on his toes. She'd heard quite enough nonsense from her young son about this dreadfully scarred woman being a witch, without him letting on to the poor soul what he and the other kids been thinking.

'I do hope you enjoyed the play!' she said quickly before Pete could finish his sentence.

'I did indeed – very much!' Dorothy answered. 'It has been such a lovely treat for me – getting out of the house for a bit . . . and seeing the children and meeting their mums. I was so grateful yesterday when your little boy invited me.'

'Yes, well, about yesterday!' said Pete's mum. She was still more than a little confused about the garbled account he'd given her at breakfast of 'spells wot really worked'. 'Our Pete said you'd cured him of the mumps and if you've really got a remedy, I'd be ever so glad to hear about it. The swelling was all but gone this morning.'

Dorothy smiled. She was tired, but very happy. Everyone was being so friendly! They had stared a bit at first, of course, but she was used to that pitying look from strangers. Now they all seemed genuinely anxious to make up for their neglect. Easter was turning out to be full of hope after all.

'I'm afraid I don't have a remedy for mumps,' she said. 'I just removed one of your little boy's teeth. I do hope you don't mind. He was very brave.'

'A tooth?' Pete's mum was beginning to understand at last. She laughed. 'Trust me to jump to the wrong conclusion! There's been a lot of mumps around this term and so I took it for granted that's what was wrong with him. I did wonder why he'd only swelled up on one side! I should've asked the doctor instead of letting him come bothering you.'

'I'm very glad you did!' Dorothy said softly.

Pete and Lee were staring at one another, trying to hide their feelings of disappointment. As if by mutual consent, they went in search of Miss Tansley.

'Aren't there really no such fings as witches and spells, Miss?' asked Pete who never doubted his teacher's unlimited fund of knowledge.

'Only in story books!' Lillian confirmed his fears.

'Nor ghosts neither?' asked Lee who shared Pete's deflation.

Pete, however, was grinning.

'Well, there's magic anyway,' he said stoutly. 'There's the magic bit where the Angel rolled the great big stone away all by hisself; and the magic where on the third day, Jesus got alive and went up to Heaven after being dead. That's a true story, isn't it, Miss?'

'Yes!' said Lillian happily. Now at least the children had an idea what Easter was all about. There was some of Pete's magic, too, in the way her play had been indirectly responsible for bringing Dorothy Amble to their notice. But for young Pete's determination to play the Angel, he would never have gone searching for a spell and . . .

Still smiling, she instructed the children to get down to the task of clearing up. All her hard work had been well worth while for, to use Pete's expression, her simple little play really had turned out to be 'a smash hit'.

Trust Me

'The number is 700 328622!'

Joanna jotted it down on the pad beside the telephone, thanked the operator and replaced the receiver.

So easy! She should have thought of it before. But then, she reminded herself, she couldn't have asked Directory Enquiries for the number of a woman whose name she did not know. It was only at the hairdresser this morning she had discovered the name of the other woman in Colin's life. The Other Woman, written in capital letters, she told herself and gave a harsh, bitter laugh.

'Calm yourself!' she thought, recognizing the hysteria that lay too near the surface of her mind. 'Have a drink and calm down, then ring up . . .'

But she was too excited to sit down. She went into the bedroom instead where she brushed her thick fair hair absent-mindedly, disarranging the morning's careful set. She stood by the window for a moment, staring into the street below. People were walking along the pavement with the seemingly aimless preoccupation of industrious ants; people she did not know and whose lives would probably never touch hers; people who lived and laughed and ate and drank and loved but who were not suffering as she was suffering at the thought of her husband in another woman's arms.

She bit her lip and clenched her hands, digging

the tapered pearl-pink fingernails into her palms. The pain was as nothing compared with the pain in her heart. It consumed her; tormented her; confused her; made the blood pump furiously in her forehead. How her head ached! In a minute she would take a couple of Disprins, maybe lie down for a while. But not yet. Not until she had telephoned. She did not need to pick up the message pad. Natalie's home number was imprinted on her mind – 700 328622.

She dialled with fingers that trembled and got the wrong number. She started to laugh when the local Chinese Take-away announced themselves; but recognizing the laughter for hysteria, she fought against it and dialled again, this time with meticulous care.

'700 328622. Hullo?' The voice was educated, rather deep, husky.

Joanna caught her breath.

'Can Mr Colin Masterton take a personal call from Edinburgh, please?' Joanna was pleased with her false voice. Her Scottish accent might well belong to an Edinburgh telephone operator. She had chosen Edinburgh because Colin's brother lived up in Scotland. Colin would assume the call had been put through from the office.

'Hold on a minute, please!'

Joanna held her breath as she listened to The Other Woman's voice calling, 'Colin? Personal call for you from Edinburgh.'

She couldn't hear Colin's reply. She didn't really need to. All she wanted to know was if he was there – with HER.

'Colin Masterton speaking!'

She couldn't, for a moment, find words. Then they came — cool, with no trace of the violent emotional reaction his voice had evoked.

'Hullo, Colin! I just wanted to be sure you were there!'

'Good God, Jo!' He couldn't have sounded more surprised, more shaken. More guilty? 'It is you, Jo, isn't it?'

'Oh, yes, it's me all right, Colin. Goodbye!'

She hung up before he could say anything more. She sat down on the bed and leaned against the pillow. She felt the sweat dampening the palms of her hands, breaking out all over her skin. For a moment or two, her whole body shook. Her mind was blank. Now that the fatal, final step was taken, she couldn't think what lay beyond it.

The telephone bell shrilling beside her, jolted her back to sanity. She knew at once it was Colin and let it ring itself into silence. She wasn't ready to talk to him — not yet!

Her mind swung backwards through the long tormented weeks of doubting, of *not knowing*, of watching Colin, judging his words, his behaviour, becoming more and more certain and yet never *quite sure*. The affair had followed what she took to be the usual pattern; Colin late back from the office; Colin wanting to go off for a weekend to see his brother in Edinburgh; Colin keeping to his own side of the double bed, finding silly little excuses to avoid kissing her, holding her hand, touching her.

'You're imagining it, Joanna!' her mother had said sternly. 'You know what you are. You've always suspected Colin's motives. I've told you before, my dear, that you'll lose him one of these days if you're jealous of every little thing in his life which excludes you. You can't possess a man utterly – he has to have some freedom.'

Joanna stared up at the ceiling, her mouth pulled into a thin, tight line. It had taken one telephone call to prove her mother wrong – a fact she'd known in her own heart. She should have tackled Colin about his secretary from that very first moment of suspicion – weeks and weeks ago. Instead, she had taken her mother's advice and said nothing, done nothing and what had it led to? A full-blooded affair.

'Joanna, you know Colin has to have a secretary and you know he needs a reasonably attractive one since she deals in the first instance with most of his clients. The fact that he says he likes her doesn't mean he's in love with her or is ever likely to be. You know he loves you, but he won't if you tear him to pieces every time he so much as smiles at another woman. Look at that dreadful scene you made over poor cousin Sally! Admit you were wrong and that Colin and Sally were completely innocent of any of the things you accused them of. And the French woman on holiday last year – no wonder Colin was so angry! You made him look an utter fool in front of her – and she almost a stranger. Do be guided by me for once in your life, Joanna, and forget this nonsense!'

The telephone rang again. This time she lifted the receiver.

'Jo? Darling, I'm nearly out of my mind. I tried to get through five minutes ago and you weren't there. Are you all right?'

'Perfectly! What did you think I was doing – putting my head in the gas oven?'

'Jo, don't talk like that. I know things look bad but I can explain everything. Honestly, darling, you must trust me. I'm coming straight home and I'll explain.'

This time she was not going to listen to Colin's explanation. His lies were always so plausible. This time she would not give him the opportunity to raise doubts, to convince her he was innocent. She would not listen.

'Are you there, Jo?' He sounded anxious . . . and with good cause, she thought bitterly.

'Oh, yes, I'm here. Where else would I be?'

'I just thought we'd been cut off . . . ' The warmth in his voice had evaporated. Now he sounded tired, uncertain of himself, *guilty? Of course* he was guilty.

'Darling, get this into your mind and hold on to it – I love you, I love *you* and no one else.'

'But not enough to be faithful!' she said bitterly and put down the receiver.

She lay quietly for a minute or two longer and then, sighing, swung her legs off the bed and sat up. Her head was spinning. It still throbbed. She would have a drink in preference to a Disprin. A brandy might stop the trembling of her limbs.

Down the passage, the door into the dining-room was ajar. She paused and stood motionless, staring in. It had taken them seven years to furnish this flat the way they wanted; seven years of marriage to build their dream home; less than ten minutes to destroy it.

She poured herself a generous measure of brandy

and the warmth stole back into her body, stimulating not only her circulation but her thoughts. Seven years! People spoke of a seven-year itch in most marriages. Had their married life begun to pall for Colin? Become dull, routine, without excitement? Was she less desirable at thirty than she had been at twenty? Colin swore she grew more attractive each passing year but then he had to say so to keep her from getting suspicious!

She walked out of the dining-room into the sitting-room. A pile of magazines lay on the coffee table. She bent and leafed through the glossy pages of one of them and gave a short laugh. How stupid, how unrealistic were some of the articles dished out to women. *How to Keep Your Husband's Love.* That was the silliest of the lot. *'Say nothing! Do nothing . . . don't force him to choose between you and the other woman . . . If he knows you know, forgive AND forget.'* As if any woman could stand idly by whilst the man she loved desperately, passionately, wholly, held another woman in his arms! As if any woman who loved her husband as she loved Colin could forgive, far less forget, such a betrayal.

'Jo!'

She hadn't heard his key in the lock. He stood in the doorway, staring at her; it seemed strange that he should be unchanged.

His eyes searched her face as if to judge her mood. Uncertain of her, he delayed the issue by going to fetch himself a drink. When he returned to the room, he saw she had not moved.

'Jo, you've just got to stop this nonsense – because that's all it is. I'm not in love with Natalie;

90

I've never kissed Natalie; I've never made love to Natalie. That's the truth and I swear it.'

She looked down into her near empty glass and sighed deeply.

'Don't make me out to be an even bigger fool than I am!' She shot him a quick angry glance. 'What else would you be doing in her flat but making love to her? You've been having an affair with her for weeks. You think I didn't know, but I did. All those nights working late at the office . . .'

'Jo, I *was* working. That I can prove if you'll give me a chance. You know how important the Waterford deal is to the firm. I explained it all to you before I began working late. And tonight, Natalie had left one of the most important files at her flat. I said I'd call in to collect it on my way home because I needed to work on it. Look, I have it here in my brief case. I'd have told you when I got home that I'd been to her place to pick it up and stopped to have a drink.'

'Would you?'

The eagerness in his face faded. He looked suddenly tired and anxious. Slowly, he sat down in the armchair.

'Maybe you're right at that. Maybe I wouldn't – but not because I had anything to hide. You make life so difficult, Jo – not just for me but for yourself. I don't understand why you can't trust me. You're jealous if I so much as say good morning to the lift girl. You've never got rid of the crazy idea that I married you for your money. So it helped buy the house and the car, *and* the partnership – but it's for us, Jo – not just for me. It's our life.

91

I love you, darling. I've always loved you, and I always will, but I don't know if I can stand much more of this. You torture yourself – and me – in a way that simply doesn't make sense. It's not as if I've ever given you any cause to suspect me.'

'Maybe not in the past, but now . . . this . . . ' her voice trailed away.

'No, you're not going to build this up into anything. If you want to know, Natalie has a boyfriend she's crazy about. He moved into her flat this spring. So you see, she wouldn't have given me a second look even if I'd done my damnedest to make her notice me. Now do you believe me?'

Joanna did not answer him. The drumming in her head had grown fiercer since she had drunk the brandy and now she was confused because Colin was there in the room with her and she loved him so much . . . *so much* . . .

'Darling!' He was coming across to her, putting his arms around her, kissing the top of her head. The throbbing was worse – a mixture of pain and pleasure.

'Jo, I beg you, darling . . . ' He drew a deep sigh – his voice reproachful as he added, 'These silly suspicions are making you ill. I'm no psychologist but I'm convinced this can be traced back to your childhood. Your mother said you always had an inferiority complex. You do believe me about Natalie, don't you? Your phoning at that moment was pure coincidence. Five minutes earlier or later and I wouldn't have been there. Or Natalie's boyfriend would have got back from work and answered the phone. Such coincidences do happen and more frequently than you might suppose. Tell me it's all all right now. Tell me you love me!'

'Yes!' she whispered. She was surprised to find tears running down her cheeks. She had not realized she was crying.

'Say you believe there's nothing between Natalie and me – nor ever has been. I want to hear you say it, darling!'

'I believe you. I'm sorry. I didn't know Natalie had a live-in lover. I'm sorry, Colin, I should have trusted you.'

He stared down at her in surprise. In the past, it had taken days to make her renew her trust in him, and even then, she had always professed herself uneasy about the future. This was new. Could she be changing at last? Her obsessive jealousy had come dangerously near to ruining their marriage.

She was smiling at him, her eyes full of love. He put his arms round her and kissed her.

'I love you!' he whispered.

'I love you, too,' she said.

'I'll nip out and get a bottle of champagne – we'll celebrate.' He kissed her again tenderly, convincingly.

Joanna walked into her bedroom to re-do her make-up. She smiled reproachfully at her reflection as she sat in front of her dressing table. How wrong her instincts had been. How *could* she have doubted his love! Her relief was total. She must never, ever doubt him again.

Out in the street, Colin turned into the nearest telephone kiosk and dialled 700 328622.

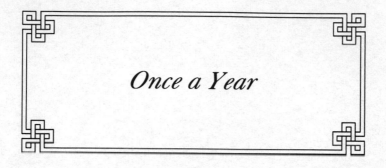

Once a Year

Muriel put down the scissors and surveyed the parcel she had been wrapping with a smile of satisfaction. It looked really pretty and the piece of red ribbon had, after all, proved to be just long enough. How thoughtful of that young girl in Hanningways to tell her it was two pence a metre cheaper in the supermarket! Shop assistants these days were often inclined to be . . . well, a little sharp and impatient, not realizing perhaps that pennies were important to people like herself who had to manage on a pension.

Today, of course, was Christmas Eve and everyone seemed as happy and excited as herself. Even the cross-faced girl at the supermarket check-out had said in a friendly voice, 'Done all your shopping then?' and when Muriel explained that her two nieces were coming to tea with her on Boxing Day, the girl had added, 'That's nice then!'

'I only see them once a year, so I like to give them a special treat!' Muriel had explained as she paid for the costly packet of chocolate biscuits and the phial of tiny silver balls with which she intended to decorate the cake she had made.

When she had had a cup of tea, she would ice the cake, Muriel decided, delaying this pleasure a little longer. Everything else was prepared – the tiny tree with its covering of tinsel and fairy lights; the freshly ironed teacloth with the green holly border which even now, after thirty years, was almost as good as new; Mother's silver-plated teapot sparkling on the sideboard. Perhaps she would give it another polish tomorrow; and since there really was nothing else to do and her bedsitter was already as clean as a new pin, she might give the teacloth another little iron.

As she stood up to fill the kettle, Muriel felt her heart flutter with excitement. The day after tomorrow, the children would be here in this very room. Not that they were really children now. Betty had written in the autumn to remind her that they were now quite grown up.

'So if you were thinking of knitting jumpers for them again this Christmas, Muriel, it really would be better not.'

Because this was such a happy day, Muriel decided not to think about the pretty blue cardigan she had already knitted for Jane with the Postman Pat motif on the pockets; nor the roll-collar jersey for Sheila with its row of Mr Men patterned over the chest. They had taken many hours of work because the patterns were intricate and her eyesight not what it had once been. Moreover wool was expensive these days – disgracefully so – and it had taken months to set aside enough twenty pence pieces from her pension to buy the quantity she had needed. It was a pity, because she loved knitting and it gave her something to do after Poor Mother had died . . .

Muriel poured out a cup of tea and went back to the chair by the window. Christmas Eve, she reminded herself, was no time to be thinking sad thoughts such as Mother's memory evoked. Even now, ten years after her death, it was difficult not to listen for Poor Mother's voice, if not explaining her needs to Muriel, then expounding her many theories on how Muriel should cope with the outside world when her mother was not there to counsel her.

What Poor Mother had failed to do, she thought not for the first time, was to advise her how to manage on a single woman's pension. Mother had intimated that she would leave Muriel and her brother 'a nice little nest egg' when she died; but when, through her tears, Muriel had finally read Mother's will, it seemed she had left everything to Gerald. Muriel had tried and finally succeeded in not feeling bitter, although at first it had seemed very unfair. Mother had always adored Gerald, the longed-for son, who was many years younger than Muriel, and who had left home as early as he could, removed himself to Yorkshire where he had married and settled down, and eventually produced two girls. He was, so he told them on his rare visits, far too busy to write or visit very often. Betty, his wife, was too busy, too. From time to time, Betty sent photographs and once a year, at Christmas, they did come. Poor Mother, being an invalid, couldn't go to visit them and Muriel, who looked after her mother, was equally housebound.

'You should put the old girl in a Home and have a holiday, Muriel,' Gerald had suggested. But he had not offered to pay for it and Mother hadn't wanted to be put in a Home; so although it was Muriel who continued to devote her life to Mother, it was the absent Gerald who was rewarded.

In time, Muriel saw that Mother was perfectly right to put Gerald first. He had two young children to bring up and a wife to support whereas Muriel had no dependants. Gerald had sold Mother's house and allowed Muriel to furnish a bed-sitting-room in Streatham with whatever pieces of family furniture she needed. It meant she could just survive on her pension.

Her one little luxury – and no longer so little these days – was her telephone. She needed it in case Gerald or Betty suddenly decided to bring the children to visit her. Once . . . it must be three or four years ago now . . . Betty had rung to say she was bringing Jane down to see a specialist about her eyes. What an exciting day that had been! It was mid summer and Betty had allowed Muriel to take the two girls down to the park whilst she went off to do a bit of shopping. They had had a lovely time on the slides and swings and the afternoon would have been quite perfect except that she hadn't had enough money to buy the children the toys they'd seen in the shop on their way home to tea. The girls had been just a tiny bit sulky and Muriel would have been more distressed had Betty not told her they had rooms full of toys at home and plenty of pocket money to buy whatever they wanted. They were very pretty girls and Muriel carried their snapshots in her purse so she could show them to anyone she chanced to meet on a walk or in a shop.

Because she did not see them very often, she had quite lost touch with their interests, Muriel reflected, and it was only natural that two young teenagers could not find their visits to her very entertaining. There had been a time when they had loved to see her – happy occasions when she

100

had played endless games of Snap and Ludo and Simon Says with them. Now, other than a nice tea and their presents, there really was nothing she could offer to amuse them.

Muriel's thin face softened into a smile. This Christmas would be different. She had put the Postman Pat cardigan and the Mr Men jersey away and by cutting down on little unnecessary items in her budget, she had saved enough to buy Trivial Pursuit.

'It's the in thing, Madam,' the shop assistant had advised. 'Right for any age, grown-ups, too, so you can't go wrong.'

It was only when she was wrapping the parcel yesterday that it occurred to Muriel the children might already have the game, but she wasn't going to worry about the possibility. This was Christmas Eve.

Across the road she could see in the light of the street lamps, the unmarried Cockney girl who lived opposite. Oddly enough, Muriel had not seen Tracey or the children for several days. From time to time, Muriel had had little chats with her. She had pushed to the back of her mind Poor Mother's cautions against becoming friendly with 'the poor'. To do so was to risk being subjected to bad language and 'even worse'; although she never elaborated on the latter. Tracey — Muriel did not know her surname — was untidy, certainly, and had one of those terrible spiky hair-styles, but she looked quite clean and her two children and the new baby seemed very well cared for. According to Tracey, the children's father had 'done a bunk' when he'd learned the new baby was on the way. 'Typical!' she had remarked

101

but with more resignation than venom in her voice. Once, when Muriel had had the flu, Tracey had seen the milk bottles left on the doorstep and taken the trouble to ring the bell and find out if she was all right. 'Thought you'd popped your clogs!' the girl had said in her jolly, friendly voice; and she'd offered to do Muriel's shopping and come in and cook her a meal.

The shrill of the telephone jolted Muriel from her seat by the window. It rang so rarely, the noise made her heart race as she picked up the receiver.

'It's Betty, Muriel . . . Gerald has a cold . . . no, not serious but he thinks it's unwise . . . so we'll have to call off our visit on Boxing Day . . . so sorry . . . another time . . . soon as we can . . . yes, we're all very disappointed, too . . . '

'Oh, dear! Oh dear, oh dear!' Muriel heard her own voice as she sat down at the table and surveyed the Christmas cake through a fuzz of unshed tears. 'Dear me! Now I really mustn't cry . . . not at Christmas . . . so selfish to think of myself when poor Gerald . . . but who will eat the chocolate biscuits? How silly I'm being! I'll have one every day with my elevenses – a nice treat, and of course, I can send the girls their Trivial game by the post . . . only a pound postage and I can manage that if . . . if . . . '

The doorbell rang.

Muriel dabbed hurriedly at her eyes. Surely the door-to-door sales people would not come calling on Christmas Eve . . . it was getting quite late. There was no one else who ever called.

She hurried to the door, patting her hair into place and giving a last dab at her eyes. 'Self

102

control,' Poor Mother used to say, 'is so important in a lady . . . '

It was Tracey – and for once, she was not smiling.

'It's the baby!' she said, white-faced. 'I'm takin' 'im to 'ospital . . . that worried . . . 'e just cries and yells and I know e's 'urting somefing awful. It's Sharon and Shirl I come about . . . '

Tracey did not feel capable of taking the girls with her to the hospital and didn't like to leave them on their own, not knowing how long she'd be away. There was no one else she could turn to but Muriel.

'I'll be as quick as ever I can!' Tracey said, looking close to tears as Muriel nodded her agreement to 'mind' the two children. 'Ever so good of you. I wouldn't never 'ave asked but . . . '

'I'll telephone for a taxi for you,' said Muriel firmly, regaining control of herself. 'And don't worry about the expense. I'll pay!'

Five minutes later, Muriel was sitting in what Tracey called her lounge, a tearful child on either side of her.

'Nobody cries at Christmas!' she said. 'And anyway, there's nothing to cry about. They'll take good care of the baby at the hospital. Now let's think of something nice to do. You've had your tea, I suppose?'

Sharon – or was it Shirl – shook her head.

Mum, the child explained, had been going to the supermarket to buy 'food and stuff' for Christmas, but with the baby ill . . .

'That settles it,' said Muriel. 'You shall come and have tea with me!'

'In your house, Miss?' the younger child asked.

'Well, I don't have a nice house like yours,' explained Muriel. 'I just have a bed-sitting-room. But I do have something nice for tea.'

They had finished the packet of chocolate biscuits, decorated and then eaten half of the Christmas cake and played two games of Snap before Muriel received the first of two further telephone calls. It was Tracey from the hospital who had thought to look up Muriel's number when she'd received no reply from her own. The baby was very poorly and the doctor wanted to keep him in overnight. Tracey could stay too, if . . .

'But of course!' said Muriel who had been so engrossed that she had not realized how late it was. 'I'll take the children home and put them to bed. Tomorrow, if you aren't back, they can have their Christmas dinner with me. Don't worry about anything, Tracey. We are enjoying ourselves.'

But Sharon – or was it Shirl – was not. As Muriel replaced the receiver, she burst into tears.

'Father Christmas won't bring us no presents if we're 'ere!' she said. ' 'ow'd 'e know where we'd gone?'

'Mum didn't have time to buy none!' the elder girl said in a whisper. She nodded in her sister's direction. 'She's a nutcase – still believes there's a Santa wot f...s around on a reindeer!'

Muriel swallowed twice and managed to retain her composure. Moreover, she had had a splendid idea.

No child had ever waited so eagerly for Christmas morning as did Muriel during that long uncomfortable night spent in an armchair in Tracey's house. The children were awake at six and roused her from a light doze.

' 'e ain't left us nuffink,' said Sharon, close to tears again.

'Then we'd better go to my place and see if he's been there!' said Muriel, savouring the moment she had been waiting for.

In the sideboard cupboard were two parcels in their bright Christmas wrappings.

'Ooh, great!' said Sharon – or was it Shirl? – as she held the cardigan against her. 'Postman Pat's me fav'rit. Brill!' Her cheeks were pink with pleasure as she struggled into it.

Shirl – or was it Sharon – was silent as she pulled the Mr Men jumper over her head.

'Fits purfick!' She looked at Muriel suspiciously. 'You couldn've knitted 'em that quick, Miss, not no way.' She paused. 'There ain't *really* a Father Christmas, is there, Miss?'

Muriel smiled.

'It was *you* who told *me* there wasn't a real one, dear!'

'Wot's in them two parcels?'

Muriel smiled as she stared down at the carefully wrapped blue and white scarf she had knitted for Gerald, and the pink mohair gloves that were to have been for Betty.

'A surprise for your Mum,' she answered, checking surreptitiously to make sure she had removed the labels.

That was when the second telephone call came. Gerald sounded . . . guilty? He certainly did not sound as if he had a cold.

'Betty said you were a bit upset when she rang

105

yesterday . . . ' he began awkwardly. 'You mustn't think we didn't want to come, but . . . '

Suddenly Muriel found herself interrupting, 'Actually, Gerald, the change of plan was fortuitous. I have unexpected visitors, you see. Now I must go as the children are waiting to open their special present . . . no, it's a game called Trivial Pursuit . . . perhaps we can chat some other time.'

Poor Mother would have said that she was being just a teeny bit uncharitable towards Gerald and Betty and the girls, but as Muriel walked firmly towards the sideboard, she really couldn't let the thought bother her. After all, she told herself, even Poor Mother had said Christmas was a time to be happy – and Christmas did only come once a year.

Goat's Loose

'I think . . .' said Kath's husband as he stood looking at the long grass in the orchard, ' . . . we should get a goat.'

Kath regarded him in astonishment. They already had two children, a baby, a dog, a cat, five kittens, three canaries, a guinea-pig and a rabbit, and her Loved One frequently complained that their house was rapidly becoming a zoo.

'To keep the grass down,' he explained.

A week later, the milkman brought them a little white billy-goat kid.

'My customer with the nanny-goat says you can have him for nothing,' he said.

'Wasn't that generous of her!' Kath remarked to her husband who said it wasn't often you got something for nothing in this life.

Kath put a collar, outgrown by their labrador, round the kid's neck, tied on a ten-foot length of rope and attached the new arrival to a tree in the garden where she could keep an eye on him. The children – and Kath – were enchanted.

'He looks just like a little white Bambi!' she said.

Half an hour later, her small daughter came running into the house.

'Goat's loose!' she said.

Goat – he was never given a real name – had eaten through the rope attaching him to the tree. He now came skipping into the kitchen via the back door, bleating pathetically. Kath gave him a crust of bread and a biscuit from the tin on the shelf. She then shut him in a shed and went down to the town to buy a dog chain.

Later that afternoon she found Goat once more in the kitchen, this time sharing the baby's teatime rusks. The baby was delighted. The spring clip attaching the new chain to Goat's collar had been wrenched open. Kath put the animal back in the shed.

Next morning she bought a new, heavier spring clip which – so the ironmonger informed her – had a spiral attachment so that the animal could not strangle itself in its attempt to get loose. At lunchtime, Kath's neighbour looked over the hedge and said, 'I happen to know a bit about goats. Billies are all right as *kids*, but when that one of yours is adult, he'll smell so dreadful you won't be able to live near him, let alone go near him. And that's not all – billy-goats are terribly fierce. They charge like bulls, you see.'

'We'd better get rid of him,' Kath told her husband that evening, by which time Goat had snapped his new leather collar, 'before it's too late.'

'But he's such a dear little chap!'

Unfortunately the only person Kath could find who was interested in taking Goat off their hands was their butcher. 'He'd make good pet food,' he said. 'On the continent, of course, humans eat goat meat. Nothing wrong with it. Yes, I'll have him.'

Kath took Goat down to the orchard. On the way there, he nuzzled her arm and licked her hand, confirming her belief that she'd made the right decision in denying him to the butcher.

Later, as she did the ironing, she switched on the radio and listened to 'Woman's Hour'.

'*Goats . . .*' said the woman speaker, ' *. . . will eat practically anything, although they don't much care for grass . . .*'

Hurriedly Kath put down the iron and ran down to the orchard. The lower levels of the two apple trees nearest Goat were shorn of their leaves, buds, blossom and bark. They looked like two would-be nudists who had decided not to go topless after all.

Remembering that she had vowed never to swear in front of the children, and that Goat was still very young, she remained silent and gazed round her. There was no more than five feet of open ground between any of the remaining apple trees.

'Bang goes our theory that he'd be handy for keeping down the grass!' she said to her husband when he arrived home.

'Never mind, darling. We'll put him in the bramble patch. That needs clearing.'

Seldom a day passed when Goat, having eaten his fill of brambles, did not manage to break loose. Kath went to the agricultural merchants and said:

'I want A VERY LARGE, STRONG CHAIN TO TETHER MY GOAT!'

The assistant produced one for her inspection.

'He'll break that in two minutes!' said Kath emphatically.

'Break it? But that's guaranteed to hold a nanny-goat,' he protested. 'I've never had any complaints . . .'

'It isn't a nanny-goat!'

111

'You mean you've got a billy?'

By this time, Kath's husband had had to pay a heavy vet's bill to have Goat neutered, and – on her neighbour's advice – dehorned at the same time, since Goat was already sporting what the children called 'a smashing pair of antlers'.

'No! He's an "it"!' she said.

The assistant disappeared and returned staggering under the weight of a length of thick, iron links.

'This is for tethering a *bull*,' he said pointedly. 'Your billy won't break this!'

He was quite right – the chain did not break, but on frequent occasions, the branch to which it was attached was snapped off. Since he could neither eat the tree nor dislodge it from the chain, Goat took it down to the kitchen with him. He knew the kitchen was the place for biscuit tins, cereal cartons, dried fruit packets and cake. He always announced his arrival by the 'clank-clank' of his chain on the path and a loud crashing noise as he butted the lid of the dustbin on his way indoors.

'Why not get an iron stake?' suggested Kath's other neighbour who viewed Goat with serious misgivings. Goat had grown alarmingly. When standing on his back legs to reach some forbidden fruit, the erstwhile kid was now at least seven foot tall. Sometimes Kath's neighbour had suddenly come face to face with Goat as they chose the same moment to look over the dividing hedge.

'An iron stake is the obvious answer!' Kath told her husband. She wondered, as she drove back from the ironmonger, why she had not thought of it before.

It took Goat three days to learn that if he ran first east to west, then north to south, in quick succession, the stake would inevitably work loose. Now he, the bull chain and the iron stake arrived together at the kitchen door.

Sometimes the children announced his coming; sometimes the phone would go and one or other of Kath's neighbours would politely inform her that it had happened again. She was never free for long from the cry: 'Goat's loose!'

They put the house up for sale. Since the new owners-to-be did not like goats, they declined to accept Kath's offer to include Goat with the carpets and fixtures and fittings at no extra cost. The day of the removal came. Goat travelled the sixty miles to his new house in the back of the estate car, his head resting lovingly on Kath's shoulder. He was unusually quiet and most unexpectedly docile. The children thought he might have been feeling car sick. Kath thought he had psychic tendencies and was somehow aware of his recent reprieve.

Not long after their removal, Kath read in a newspaper an article by a retired major living in the West Country. In it, he described his experiences when starting up a sanctuary for domestic pets – to keep himself active when he left the Army, he explained.

My wife and I love all animals and are pre-pared to offer any unwanted pets a home – anything from a canary to a goat. We are particularly fond of goats who can be very intelligent animals . . .

*

113

Kath felt a stir of excitement. She took the newspaper article downstairs and put it on the kitchen unit to show her husband when he came home. In the two years since Goat's arrival, the only offer of adoption they had had was from the butcher. Now, no doubt, even the butcher would consider him too tough to be eaten . . . since Goat had attained at least twice the strength of a Shetland pony.

Kath went about her day's work singing. Goat, she decided, must have sensed something was in the wind. Today he neither pulled up his stake nor gave any trouble when she went down to the field to move him. More often than not, when she loosened the stake he would make a dive for the house or the orchard, jerking her off her feet and swinging her on the end of his chain towards the duck pond. Today, he nuzzled against her, licked her hand and pushed his bearded face into her chest with playful little butts.

Kath steeled her heart.

At tea-time, her son called her in from the garden.

'Goat's in the kitchen!'

She raced indoors and found Goat happily munching cereal he had shaken loose from the packet. He stood in a sea of Sugar Pops, smiling. Kath swore he was smiling, although when she told her husband later, he said:

'I don't think goats can smile!' Then, to cheer her up: 'Never mind, darling, he'll be the major's problem soon.'

But he wasn't. Before Goat had found the Sugar Pops, he had found the newspaper cutting – the all-important article from the retired major in the

West Country. He'd left one small corner – not the corner with the address on it, but the one on which was written:

We're particularly fond of goats . . .

Kath wrote to the newspaper asking them to send her the major's name and address. Either their reply was lost in the post or in one of Goat's three stomachs. In any event, she never received one.

Eleven years later, Kath and her husband were obliged to have Goat put to sleep. He had lost all his teeth in his old age – due to too much sweet stuff – the vet said. Kath's husband disagreed. Sugar Pops had never done the children any harm so he didn't think a handful now and again could possibly have hurt poor old Goat. He was very upset.

That was over a year ago and Kath is still mourning for Goat. Sometimes she thinks she can hear the rattling of the biscuit tin, or the 'clank-clank' of his chain by the back door. It's strange how fond she and her husband were of that animal. She freely admits that she would give her right arm to hear someone calling on the telephone to tell her: 'Goat's loose!'

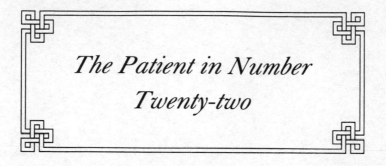

The Patient in Number
Twenty-two

'It isn't too late to change your mind, Pippa!'

Sue looked anxiously at her cousin. Framed by the delicate, creamy lace bridal veil, Phillipa's tense face was paper white, her brown eyes two dark, unnaturally bright pools. Her hands clutched her bouquet so tightly that the knuckles too, showed white beneath the pale, pink skin.

Fearing that the stems of the lilies and orange blossom would be crushed, Sue gently eased the clenched fingers.

'Pippa, listen to me! Charles wouldn't be the first bridegroom to be left standing at the altar – and if you don't really love him – well, he'd be grateful in the end . . . '

Her uncle's voice calling to Sue to hurry, interrupted her. The car taking her and her aunt to the church was waiting for them.

'I'm going to have to leave, Pips.' Nevertheless, Sue paused, laying a hand gently on her cousin's shoulder. 'Darling, I meant it – it isn't too late.' Phillipa's whole body was trembling. 'I'll go down and explain to your parents. You can stay here . . . I'll cope with everything.'

Phillipa stood up, the long shining folds of her satin wedding dress falling gracefully around her thin figure.

'Thanks, but I'm going to go through with it – I'm going to marry Charles.'

'Fine! Then I'd better dash.' Sue bent and

kissed her cousin's cheek. Despite its pallor, it was burning hot. 'Best of luck, darling! See you at the church!'

Phillipa sat down once more at her dressing-table.

'It's not too late,' Sue had said, but it was, much much too late ever to know the kind of happiness she should be feeling now. It was five years too late . . .

She listened to the sound of the car driving away down the street. Now they were alone in the house – her father and herself. He, like Mother, was so pleased about this marriage. 'Charles is such a splendid fellow,' Father kept saying; and, 'you and Charles are so perfectly matched, so well suited to one another!'

He was right, of course.

Through the open window, she could hear her father telling the chauffeur of the bridal car that she would be ready in a few minutes. Somehow she must stop this terrible trembling; the shivering. Her head throbbed, which was hardly surprising, she thought, seeing that she had hardly slept last night, and when she had, her dreams had tormented her.

She reached for the glass of water and Disprin Sue had left on her dressing-table and took two of the tablets. A little of the water splashed on her dress – such a beautiful dress, she thought sadly! Mother had insisted upon having it specially made at Harrods – no expense spared. Everyone agreed it was beautiful; that she looked beautiful in it. Keith would want to take a photo of her wearing it – but he wouldn't ever see it. He had refused the invitation to the wedding.

120

'For God's sake, Pippa, you don't honestly think I want to be there, do you? Damn Charles Witherborn; damn you, Phillipa. And do me a favour – don't come to my flat again!'

Later, he had rung up to apologize; begged her to meet him somewhere – to talk things over; vowed he wasn't going to give up hope until she was actually married.

'I love you! I'll never stop loving you! And I don't believe you really love that . . . that Yuppie, Charles.'

'I do, I do!' she had reiterated, but as Keith said, you couldn't love two men. Yet she loved Keith – for different reasons, of course – every bit as much as she loved Charles. Why, then, had she chosen Charles in the end?

'Phillipa? The car's waiting. We should be going.'

Glancing in the mirror, Phillipa noticed with surprise that tears were coursing down her cheeks. She had not been aware she was crying. She tried to wipe them away, but they kept falling, dripping on to her bouquet, her hands, leaving little, dark patches on her lap.

Vaguely, she heard her father calling her again. He sounded impatient and she knew she must hurry although for the moment, she had forgotten where she was going. Never mind, she told herself, Father will tell me. I must hurry.

Dropping her bouquet in her haste, she went quickly out on to the landing. Far down below, her father was standing at the foot of the stairs. She was surprised to see that he was wearing striped trousers, a grey top hat; that he had a white carnation in his button hole.

121

'Phillipa, will you please get a move on, darling. We're five minutes late already!'

'I'm coming, Father. I was just . . . I was trying . . . I wanted . . . '

She took a step forward and then, as everything began to revolve around her, she felt herself falling, falling, as if in slow motion, down the stairs.

FRIDAY

The two nurses relaxed as they sat in the rest room taking a welcome ten-minute break. Katy, the more senior, put down her cup of cocoa and smiled at the younger girl.

'You've been here a week now, Gwen. Think you're going to like it?'

'It's fascinating. It's the variety of patients which I enjoy.'

Katy nodded.

'Oh, you get all sorts in a private clinic like this. You certainly can gain experience here.'

'Which is why my parents were so keen I took the job. I want to specialize in mental nursing but my parents don't like the idea of me being in that kind of environment. I realize it must be a great drain on the emotions – but my sister is a Down's Syndrome child, you see, so I've always been interested in mental illness. Anyway, I promised my parents I'd try other types of nursing before I made any firm decisions – so here I am.'

The older woman nodded.

'Sounds very sensible. So you'll be interested in

Phillipa Armstrong, the girl in Number Twenty-two.'

'I was looking at her notes. She's the same age as me. Matron said she was admitted as an amnesiac, but I gather there's more to it – that it's self-induced?'

'Dr Morton thinks it is. You see, she remembers perfectly well who her parents are – and those two chaps who've wanted to visit her. If she really didn't remember them, she wouldn't be so adamant that she doesn't want to see them.'

Gwen grinned.

'I saw the dark-haired one – rivals Mel Gibson!'

Katy laughed.

'If I'd been a year or two younger, I'd have fancied the tall fair-haired one myself. One wonders why the poor girl is so unhappy. Sometimes when I go into her room, she's sitting in that chair by the window with tears pouring down her cheeks. She doesn't seem to realize she's crying.'

The younger nurse sighed.

'The way she sits there all day nursing that Walt Disney rabbit thing made me wonder if she'd lost a baby or had an abortion recently.'

Katy shook her head.

'The doctors say not.'

'She's very pretty. She let me wash and blow-dry her hair yesterday and you could see that with a little more weight, she'd be quite stunning. She's fearfully thin.'

'Apparently they had to feed her intravenously after the accident. The poor girl had a fractured skull – and a broken collar bone. She was in a coma for three weeks but they kept her in the hospital for ages, partly to give the fractures time to mend, but there was also this problem of her refusing to talk. This past ten days, she's been here at the clinic under observation, but they can't find anything physically wrong. Dr Morton's taking her on – he's our psychiatrist. By the way, Matron did tell you to talk to her as much as possible, didn't she?'

'Yup! And to record anything she says. So far all I've had has been "yes", "no" and "thank you".'

Katy stood up.

'Better get back to work.' She put down her empty mug and added reassuringly, 'We all think Dr Morton's brilliant. If anyone can find out what's wrong with Phillipa Armstrong, he will. I said as much to her parents. The poor dears are worried to death about her. They know she could regress. It's one thing to withdraw voluntarily from a world you don't like, but the brain is a funny thing – it could reach a point when she couldn't get back to normal even if she wanted. At her age, that could be a tragedy.'

'Then she's lucky to have parents who can afford to keep her here. It must be costing them an absolute packet.'

'Perhaps they're on BUPA!' Katy said. 'Now get a move on, Gwen. We aren't paid the kind of salaries we're getting to sit and gossip all day.'

'You sound like Matron!' Gwen said laughing as she followed the senior nurse out of the room.

MONDAY

'Do sit down, Phillipa. I may call you by your first name?'

124

She nodded, her face impassive.

'Let me introduce myself. I'm Dr Morton – Edwin Morton – your psychiatrist. I hope we're going to be good friends as we'll probably be seeing a lot of each other over the next few weeks.'

'Aren't I going home then?' Phillipa asked. 'Sister said I was better – much better.'

'Indeed you are, Phillipa. That's why you're here. You know you've had a breakdown, don't you? We want to make sure it doesn't happen again.'

'Sister said something about a nervous breakdown. I don't really remember . . . it's funny, you look a bit like Charles, only your voice is different.'

'So you remember Charles?'

Phillipa looked away from his face and down at her hands. They were, she noticed in that strange, detached way by which she seemed to become aware of things since she'd been ill, gripped together. It was almost as if each hand was trying to hold on to the other.

'Phillipa, look at me, will you? I'd like you to tell me about Charles. Who is he?'

Phillipa frowned.

'Surely someone has told you that. He's my husband, of course!'

The doctor picked up a sheaf of notes and glanced through them.

'Sister says a Mr Charles Witherborn has been sending flowers every day – and that he was most anxious to see you.'

'Has he?' Phillipa's voice was vague. 'I don't remember.'

'You haven't been well enough to receive visitors. Now about Charles . . . '

I don't in the least want to talk to this strange man about Charles. He seems to think it's important although I can't see why. It's not as if I'm still feeling ill. Perhaps he'll let me go home if I tell him what he wants to know. I don't know what I'm doing here but at least it's better sitting in this comfortable chair than lying under that brain scan thing and having needles stuck into me and pills shoved down my throat. Sister said it was the right treatment seeing that I'd fallen down a whole flight of stairs. I don't remember falling. I . . . Oh, God, he's on about Charles again. I'll give him my best smile. It seems to please everyone in this place if I smile.

'Charles Anthony Witherborn – how's that for a good memory, Doctor?'

He doesn't look very impressed – I'll have to do better or go to the back of the class! Don't giggle, Phillipa. He'll think you're bonkers. I suppose you are bonkers. People who have mental breakdowns . . . All right, I heard you, Doctor.

'Charles is my husband and father of my baby.'

That took the wind out of his sails!

'I didn't know you had a child, Phillipa.'

'Oh, yes. After all, that's one of the main reasons I married Charles. I wanted a baby, preferably a son, and Charles gave me one. He always gives me everything I want. He's very rich – what you'd call "frightfully well off".'

I thought my Yuppie accent was rather good. No sense of humour, this man. This is really a waste of time, his and mine.

'So having this baby made you very happy?'

'Obviously! Charles wasn't too pleased at first – I

mean, we'd only been married three months when I got pregnant. He wanted me all to himself – we were very sociable, you see; and then Charles was very keen on sex.'

That made him look up from his notes! He is a doctor, when all's said and done, so why the surprise?

'He organized a nanny – so I'd be free when he wanted me. Charles has always wanted his life to run on oiled wheels. He can afford to make it do so, so why not? He's very easy going. I expect you'd like him – most people do. He's very charming – and good-looking. He's one of those people you never pick a fight with because he doesn't believe there's all that much worth fighting about. We never argue.'

'About the baby – your little son. What is his name?'

'I can't think why you want to know. He's called Henry. Charles wanted his son to be named after him, and I wanted him to be called Rab. Anyway, we compromised and called him Henry after my father. Look, Doctor, I'm tired, and my head aches. Do we have to go on with this?'

'Of course not! We'll talk again tomorrow, Phillipa. Before you go, is there anything you want to ask me?'

She paused at the doorway.

'As a matter of fact, there is. Am I mad? I mean, I really would like to know. I'm somewhat confused.'

'Of course you are. In the first place, you fell down a whole flight of stairs and hit your head, as a consequence of which you suffered a certain amount of amnesia. You were also at the time of your fall, suffering a mild breakdown. The mind

127

can get ill as well as the body, you know. You had a hairline fracture of the skull which has healed very nicely; but we've yet to discover the reason why you've made so little effort to regain your memory.'

'I don't know what you're talking about. There's nothing the matter with my memory. What makes you say there is? If that's the only reason you are keeping me in this stupid place, then you're wasting your time. Sister said it was a private clinic. I suppose you're charging huge fees for keeping me here and that's why you are refusing to let me go home.'

That was pretty rude of me, but he isn't looking angry.

'You must learn to trust me, Phillipa. Here's Sister to take you back to your room. We'll meet again soon.'

WEDNESDAY

'You're looking very attractive today, Phillipa. New hairstyle?'

That's a pretty familiar remark coming from someone who's almost a complete stranger. It's all very well for Sister to say I had a long chat with this Dr Morton last week, but I can't honestly say I remember much about it, other than that I didn't like him. Counselling sessions, Sister calls them, to help me get well again. I must find out if they are compulsory . . .

'Are you quite comfortable in that chair? Just relax! There's nothing to worry about. Let's see now, we were talking last week about your husband, Charles!'

128

'You've got it all wrong. Charles is just a friend – an ex-boyfriend, if you like. My husband's name is Keith. He's an author – quite a good one, actually, though he doesn't make any money at it!'

'Ah, Keith. Nice name! Tell me about him.'

'I can't think why it should interest you, but since you ask, he's terribly good-looking. Henry's very like him to look at.'

'Henry?'

'Our little boy. Now he's really something. When we go shopping, everyone stops to admire him. I suppose it's not surprising Keith gets jealous!'

'Does he?'

'He's bound to, isn't he? After all, I do have to give Henry most of my time. Babies are terribly demanding when they're small. Keith wanted me to have an abortion when I got pregnant. We couldn't afford a baby – or much else, come to that. Most of the time, we were on social security. I had to give up my job when Henry was born, you see. Not that lack of money ever worried Keith. He just wanted us to be alone together.'

'So you wanted the baby, but Keith didn't?'

'Well, you couldn't really expect him to, could you? Writers need peace and quiet, and we only had the one room and our bedroom. My father wanted to lend us the money to buy a house – but he and Keith never hit it off and Keith was too proud to let my parents subsidize us.'

'How did you feel about that?'

'I suppose I understood really. After all, both my parents made it pretty obvious they disapproved of Keith from the word go. They're very old-fashioned and had a fit when I moved in with

129

Keith – to live with him. I don't suppose we would have got married if it hadn't been for the baby.'

'What had your parents got against Keith? They must have been aware that you loved him.'

I simply don't see the point of all these questions. It really isn't any of his business. I wish he'd just leave me alone.

'If you must know, they'd set their hearts on me marrying Charles. They would, wouldn't they? I mean, Charles was rolling in it and could give me everything I might possibly want.'

'Tell me about Charles.'

'I've just told you, he was my boyfriend before I met Keith. He was enormously eligible. I didn't live with him . . . or sleep with him. I don't know why not. He's nice looking . . . Mother used to say "distinguished-looking", which I suppose is true. He's very athletic, good at tennis and squash and all that. He has a villa in the South of France and he took me there one summer. It was lovely. We went with some friends of his who had a yacht. I nearly did sleep with him, as a matter of fact. I would have . . . only by then I'd met Keith. It was one of those physical things with Keith. We couldn't keep our hands off each other. A sort of instant attraction. I was pretty young – and, believe it or not – a virgin. Keith was a wonderful lover and it was all wonderful until . . .'

'I think that's enough for today, Phillipa. You're looking tired. We'll talk some more soon, shall we? By the way, Sister said your parents have been asking to visit you. How do you feel about that?'

I've told Sister . . . I've told her I don't want to see them. I'm not a child. I'll manage my life the way I

130

want. Just because I've not been well . . .

'Why can't you all leave me alone? Talk, talk, talk – there's no peace.'

'Everyone wants to help you get well, Phillipa. I know you'd rather not communicate with anyone, but we can't allow you to shut yourself away from the world.'

'Why can't you? I'm not being a nuisance to anyone. All I want is to be left alone. I'm perfectly happy when I'm left alone, but there's always some stupid nurse interrupting me just when . . . just when . . . talk, talk, talk. That's all they do, interrupting me . . .'

'Don't worry about it, Phillipa. Believe me, we are all trying to help you get better and you won't do that by keeping your thoughts locked up inside your head. Try and trust me. You *are* getting better although it may not seem so to you. Now be a good girl and just do as the nurses tell you. Sister said you were refusing to take your pills last night.'

I'm not going to talk to him. He can't make me. Tomorrow I'll get out of this place. Just as soon as I've made up my mind where I want to go, I'll leave. They treat me like a silly child. I'm not silly! It's those pills which are silly . . . which make me cry.

'I'll see you tomorrow, Phillipa, when you're feeling better.'

I'll never feel better. I'll never, ever be happy again.

THURSDAY

'I see you are not alone today, Phillipa!'

'Sister said I could bring him.'

'But of course. He's a rather unusual rabbit, isn't he — not exactly rabbit shaped.'

'I nearly didn't bring him. I thought you might think me stupid.'

'Why should I do that?'

'A grown woman walking around with a soft toy . . .'

'Lots of adults have mascots. Does he have a name?'

'He's called Rab — not very original, I'm afraid.'

'It's nice to see you smiling. Are you feeling happy today?'

'Yes, I am, as a matter of fact.'

'Did you make Rab yourself?'

'Oh, no. My mother gave him to me for my sixth birthday. I had such a lot of dolls, you see, so she thought a toy rabbit would make a change.'

'But mostly you played with your dolls?'

'I suppose so. Sue — she's my cousin — liked my dolls best, but Alan liked Rab.'

'I don't think I know who Alan is.'

'A boy I used to know. His parents had a cottage in the same road. He was only a year older than me, so if he hadn't anything better to do, he'd come round to our house to play.'

'Just the two of you?'

'Sometimes Sue came, too. She and I were more like sisters than cousins. Her mother was a semi-invalid and so Sue often came to live with us in the holidays.'

'Where is Sue now?'

'She married a Canadian and went to live in Toronto years ago.'

'So it's a long time since you last saw her?'

'I don't know. I can't remember. Is it important?'

'Let's talk about something else. What kind of games did you play?'

'The usual – "mothers and fathers" when we were little. Rab was our baby. We built a house once at the end of the garden. Alan made some chairs and a table – when he was older, of course – and we had picnics there in summer.'

'How old would Alan have been then?'

'I don't know – ten or eleven. He was doing woodwork at school – that's why he liked making things for the house.'

'And was Rab still your baby?'

'Oh, no. We'd outgrown "mothers and fathers" by then. But we still played with Rab. Look, do you really want to know all this?'

'I wouldn't be asking if I wasn't interested, Phillipa. Now you're smiling again. Can you tell me why?'

'I was just remembering. Alan had a bow and arrows – not real ones, but those things with rubber plungers on the end. We tied a string on Rab and I had to run round the garden pulling him whilst Alan tried to shoot him. He got quite good at it. I was hopeless! Poor old Rab got a bit dog-eared in those days and Mother had to repair him. When Alan's father came home – he was in the Navy so he was usually abroad somewhere – he taught Alan how to shoot a real airgun, so after that, we didn't play with the bow and arrows any more. Alan shot at tin cans and we stopped using Rab as a target.'

'Was Sue, your cousin, included in these games?'

'Sometimes! We played different kinds of games. I mean, you can't have two mothers and only

133

one father, can you? So we made it "brides and grooms" and Sue was the bridesmaid or the vicar. Or we'd play "hare and hounds" and Alan would be the hare and we'd have to catch him. If it was raining, we'd go indoors and play dressing-up, or Monopoly or Ludo. When Alan and I were on our own, we used to play chess or backgammon. We always found something to do.'

'So you had a very happy childhood?'

'Oh, yes I did! Although I was an only child, I was never lonely. There was always Sue or Alan to play with. Sue and I were closer than some sisters.'

'So you were sad when she married and went to live so far away?'

'I missed her terribly, but perhaps not as much as I would have done if I'd been younger. I mean, I was growing up and I had my own life to lead. At least she was married in England and I was able to be her bridesmaid. We'd made each other a promise when we were kids – that neither of us would get married unless the other was there to be a bridesmaid.'

'So Sue was to be your bridesmaid?'

I think I'm getting one of my bad headaches. It's all this talking. I was feeling perfectly all right when I came in here. I wish I could remember who this man reminds me of. I really don't like him. He has a horrible looking wart by his left ear. Alan used to say ogres had warts all over their bodies but I don't know if that's really true. There was a picture of one in that Weird Tales *book Alan's uncle gave me. We . . .*

'Phillipa, you do want to get well, don't you? I can't make you better without your help. You do want to help me, don't you? Your mother and

134

father are very worried about you. It's natural they should worry about their only child. They love you very much.'

'I can't help that, can I? Anyway, you said I wasn't ill.'

'Not physically, Phillipa, although you are very underweight. Shall we go on with our talk?'

'No, I don't want to. I've got a headache. I want to go back to my room. If you want me to be frank, I don't really like you very much. I'm sorry if that sounds rude – but Sister said that all you wanted was for me to tell the truth.'

'Sister's quite right! I hope she also told you that you can trust me? I happen to think you are a very special person and although you don't like me, I want us to be friends. Now you are smiling again. I'd like to know why.'

'I was just thinking about us – being friends, I mean. Blood brothers, like Sue and Alan and me. We cut our fingers with Alan's penknife and mixed our blood. Kids are stupid sometimes, aren't they?'

'If you feel like it, Phillipa, I'd like you to do something for me before we see each other tomorrow. Will you write a letter to Sue? I know she's aware of your accident, but I think she'd like to hear from you – that you're getting better.'

'But I'm not, am I?'

'I think you are! Don't worry about it, Phillipa. Just trust me!'

'You're always saying that – it's such a bore!'

'I'll see you tomorrow. Bring Rab again. I can see he's really rather special.'

How silly this man is! Calls himself a specialist, too! Any fool could see Rab's only a soft toy. What's so special

135

about that, for goodness sake? I don't think I'll come here
tomorrow, and if I do, I shan't bring Rab.

MONDAY

'Do sit down, Phillipa. Make yourself comfortable.
I see our nice new nurse brought you here today.
Don't you like her? She tells me you won't talk to
her.'

'I don't feel like talking!'

'But you do want to get better, don't you? Last
week, you were telling me about your marriage –
and your little boy. Henry, wasn't it?'

'Oh, he's fine! Nanny says he has cut some more
teeth, and he started walking while we were away.'

'You went away?'

'Charles took me skiing – to Davos. I wanted
to take Henry but Charles said that would mean
taking Nanny, too, and none of our friends were
taking their children.'

'Was it a good holiday?'

'I suppose so! I did learn to ski – after a fashion.
Eva's frightfully good . . . black runs no problem.'

'I don't think you've mentioned Eva before. Was
she one of the party you went with?'

'Naturally! Her brother, Tim, is Charles' best
friend. Everyone thought Eva and Charles would
get married one day. It's perfectly obvious she's in
love with him, but Charles says that's rubbish. Not
that I mind!'

'You're not jealous then?'

'Why should I be? I'm the one Charles chose to
marry. He's the one who's jealous.'

136

'Do you give him cause to be?'

'Of course not! But he knew about my affair with Keith. I suppose everyone did since we were living together.'

'You continued to see Keith then – after you'd met Charles?'

'Not deliberately, but we ran into each other occasionally. Keith writes books and when he finally had a book accepted for publication, I went to the launch. It would have been churlish not to, wouldn't it? We had dinner together afterwards. Charles was furious.'

'Did you quarrel about it?'

'Not really! Charles isn't the type to enjoy a row. The only thing he gets really upset about is when I won't sleep with him. Mostly I do when I know he wants to make love, but sometimes . . . I just don't feel like it.'

'Do you know why?'

'Not really! I'm just not all that keen on sex. And anyway, I'm usually too tired. I mean, we're always at parties or giving them. Quite often, I overdo the drinking and by the time I fall into bed, I just pass out.'

'You enjoy drinking?'

'Not particularly! I suppose I drink to give me a lift. I'm not really into the social roundabout. We have to do it, because of Charles' work. It's an important part of his job to make contacts and keep in touch. The people we see – they aren't really friends. It's all so superficial.'

'So you aren't very happy?'

'I've no right to be anything else. I have everything I want. Charles gives me a free rein and there

are no financial restrictions. I have a lovely home –
it's really beautiful! A nice garden; my own BMW;
a wardrobe full of lovely clothes; and of course,
I've got Henry – and Nanny to look after him.'

'No regrets then? Your career, for instance. I
believe you were taking A levels with a view to
going to veterinary college?'

'Oh, that! That was years ago – when I was a
teenager. It was a silly idea. I was very immature
for my age. Anyway, my parents weren't at all keen
on the idea. They are very old-fashioned. Mother,
in particular, didn't think it a suitable career for a
girl.'

'So she was pleased when you decided not to
go to college?'

'Not really! You see, I met Keith that summer
after my A level results and went up to London
to live with him. I was eighteen, so my parents
couldn't stop me.'

'Can you tell me why you married Charles? Was
it to please your parents?'

'I don't know! Why does one get married?
Things weren't working out too well with Keith
and Charles was pursuing me. I wanted . . . I
wanted a baby and I knew if I married Charles
we could afford a family, have a nice home – that
kind of thing. Everyone liked him. I did. It's nice
to be wanted by someone the way Charles wanted
me. It wasn't just bed, you see, the way it was with
Keith. In fact, I didn't fancy Charles all that much
although he is very good-looking. It was just very
nice being with him – being spoilt, for one thing;
and then there were no emotional ups and downs.
When you were in his company, it was like drifting

along on the surface of a calm sea. He's the most equable person I've ever known. I think that's why people get on so well with him. He's very easy to live with.'

'So you do still love him?'

'I don't know what you mean by love. If you mean the stupid sort of romantic nonsense people write about in cheap novels, then no, I don't love Charles. I don't believe that kind of thing exists – except in stories. When you get down to real life, you wake up to the fact that it's nothing but a fairy-tale. Like Father Christmas. No, that kind of love is just a figment of the imagination.'

'You sound very certain. Is it possible you could be wrong?'

'No, it isn't possible. And I don't really want to argue the point with you. If you're really so naïve as to believe in that one-man, one-woman myth, you're welcome to do so. I happen to know I'm right. Can I go back to my room now? It's probably time for my pills, and Gwen said that after my session with you, she'd make me a cup of tea.'

'Then I won't detain you, Phillipa. I'll see you same time tomorrow.'

'If you must – though frankly, I think you are wasting your time.'

TUESDAY

'I hear you had a bad night, Phillipa! I hope you aren't feeling too tired to talk?'

139

'The night nurse gave me a sleeping pill.'

'I understand you were having some bad dreams. Can you remember them?'

'No, I can't!' *And anyway, I don't see the point in reliving nightmares. I suppose I'll have to say something or he'll accuse me of not co-operating.* 'If they were bad dreams, they probably involved the break up of my marriage to Keith.'

'I thought you were just living with him – that's Keith, the author, isn't it?'

'That's right! Everything was fine before we were married. We were madly in love. Perhaps I should say, passionately in love. We couldn't leave each other alone. It was one of those things. We seldom got as far as the double bed. We'd make love anywhere, on the floor, in the bath, up against the kitchen sink, on the stairs.' *I bet that's given him something to think about!* 'I hope I haven't shocked you!'

'It isn't a doctor's job to moralize, Phillipa. My job is to help you come to terms with your problems.'

'I don't have any problems.'

'We were talking about Keith, your marriage?'

'Yes, well that was a mistake. We had to get married because of the baby. I told you I got pregnant, didn't I? Having Henry put me off sex. Keith didn't understand. He hated it when I went down to stay with my parents. He knew they didn't approve of him and he refused to come with me when I went home. He hated country life – whereas I was perfectly happy tramping round the fields and woods with my dog. Then there was Charles . . .'

'Charles?'

140

'Keith called him my lover, but he wasn't – not then. He was just an ex-boyfriend who'd wanted to marry me. I ran into him in Harrods where I'd been doing some shopping for my mother and he invited me to lunch. I had nothing to hide, so I told Keith. He was furious – quite absurdly jealous. I suppose that's when things really started to go wrong. We'd row and Keith would storm out of the flat and not come back for days.'

'That worried you?'

'Not really! It was quite nice to have a bit of peace and quiet. Anyway, he'd always come back in the end. We'd make up and make love and so it would go on till the next time. Until I found out about Fiona.'

'Found out what?'

'That whenever Keith walked out on me, he went round to her. I suppose I should have guessed something of the sort would happen. Keith blamed me – saying he wouldn't have needed to have sex with Fiona if I'd not refused him. He promised to give her up – but he didn't. So I left him. I shouldn't ever have married him. The only thing we had in common was this physical attraction thing, and when that wore off, there wasn't anything else.'

'You'd not suspected this before you went to live with him?'

'I may have done. I don't remember. I don't suppose it would have made any difference if I had known. At that point in my life, all I wanted was to get away from home.'

'Weren't you happy at home? You told me you loved country life.'

'Did I? Look, Dr Morton – I know you're trying

141

to help me, but I really can't understand why. I'm not ill. So I had a nervous breakdown – but I'm perfectly all right now. Or I am until you start asking me all these questions. What does it matter what happened in the past? It all went wrong and that's all there is to it. Why can't I go home?'

'We'll see, Phillipa. You are getting better and perhaps in a week or two . . . you'll just have to trust me. And Phillipa, before you go, I want to ask you to do something for me. You have a very vivid imagination and sometimes I think you lose sight of what is real and what is in your imagination. Next time we talk, I want you to tell me the truth.'

'So you think I've been telling you lies!'

'That's something you will have to decide for yourself. I'll see you tomorrow.'

WEDNESDAY

'Do you remember what I asked you to do for me today, Phillipa!'

'Of course I do. There's nothing wrong with my memory! I'm to tell you the truth, the whole truth and nothing but the truth!'

'You're a very pretty girl when you smile, but I expect you're well aware of it. How old were you when you first woke up to the fact that you were attractive?'

'What an odd question! In my teens, I suppose. I was still at school, studying for my A levels. Did I tell you I wanted to be a vet? Alan was already at veterinary college and as soon as we'd both qualified, we were going to set up in practice together.

142

We were both mad about animals and neither of us wanted to work in an office, so it seemed the obvious thing to do.'

'So you were sixteen? Seventeen?'

'About that! Sue and I used to get asked out by the boys in the sixth form – swimming, roller-skating, the cinema – that kind of thing. It was all pretty juvenile, nothing serious. We were very into hairstyles, fashions, make-up; fancied ourselves as sirens rather than schoolgirls! But I suppose we did look different. When Alan came home for the summer, he hardly recognized us. We went out a lot that summer – Alan and a friend of his called Bob, and Sue and me. I think it was the happiest summer of my life.'

'Did you find Alan attractive?'

'Who wouldn't? It wasn't so much that he was particularly good-looking. He had sandy hair, and freckles and he wasn't very tall – but there was something special about him. Everyone liked him. Of course, I'd always adored him – hero-worshipped him the way little girls do with older brothers. That summer, though, it was different. I thought I was in love with him – typical teenage crush! It was a 'first' for both of us, although we didn't – as Mother would put it – go all the way! Just as well, really, seeing we were both to end up with different partners.'

'But you thought then that it was for real?'

'Oh, yes, we both did. Alan invited me up to Edinburgh to his college Christmas dance. It sounds quite ridiculous now, but he gave me a ring from one of the crackers and said we were engaged; that he'd get me a proper ring as soon

143

as I'd left school. We both knew my parents would throw a fit if I'd said I was going to marry him.'

'I thought your parents liked Alan!'

'They did! But I was only sixteen and Alan eighteen. We were very young.'

'So you were secretly engaged. What went wrong?'

'Wrong? Well, for one thing, before Alan graduated, his uncle died and left his sheep ranch in New Zealand to Alan. Alan went out there to see what it was all about, fell in love with the country and stayed there.'

'And you?'

'Well, my parents were very keen for me to take my A levels. I'd only a year to go, so it did make sense. Alan thought so, too, so we planned for me to go out to New Zealand and join him the following year. My parents kicked up an awful fuss when I told them. Being an only child, they couldn't bear the thought of me leaving England and going to live on the other side of the world. Of course, they knew they couldn't stop me going as I'd be eighteen by then. They were pinning their hopes on Charles.'

'Charles being . . . ?'

'The eldest son of one of their local friends. We'd met at a hunt ball the Christmas after Alan went away.'

'I think you told me about Charles – a very wealthy, eligible young man.'

'All of that! I suppose I was the only girl around who wasn't chasing him. I liked him well enough, but I was in love with Alan – or thought I was. That didn't stop Charles proposing practically every time we met. I don't have to tell you, my parents were encouraging him like mad!'

'So what happened when you got your A levels?'

'I didn't! I flunked them – all of them!'

'Do you know why?'

'I suppose I just hadn't done the groundwork. I'd had other things to think about . . . '

'Your future in New Zealand?'

'Didn't I tell you? That was all off. Alan had met another girl – and I'd met Keith. You've got to remember how young we both were when Alan went away. We were only kids and . . . well, you grow up and grow apart. We used to write to each other at first, but gradually the weekly letters became monthly ones, and sometimes there were even longer gaps because Alan was fearfully busy. That was when I suspected he was falling in love with Sandra. She was the farm manager's daughter so Alan saw a great deal of her. His letters were full of things they'd done together around the ranch. I was still nurturing my adolescent dreams and so convinced myself Alan was telling the truth when he wrote that he and Sandy were just friends. I told myself everything would be OK when he came home.'

'He was coming back to England?'

'That's right. He was taking a month's holiday to coincide with my leaving school. Then he wrote to say Sandy's father had died and he couldn't get away. I started wondering again if everything was over between us.'

'Was it?'

'Not exactly! My parents had given me some money for my eighteenth birthday so I decided I'd fly over to see Alan as he couldn't come to see me. I even booked a flight. But when I

145

telephoned him to tell him, he wasn't there. I spoke to Sandy's aunt who said Alan and Sandy had gone skiing together. I told her I'd rung to say I was planning to visit Alan in June and said I would ring again, although I was hoping Alan would ring me. He didn't! A week later, I swallowed my pride and rang again. This time the aunt told me Alan and Sandy had gone to Wellington and were staying overnight. That was when I finally got the message – he'd found someone else he loved more than me.'

'So you broke off the engagement?'

'Well, it was never a real one, was it? Anyway, by that time, I'd met Keith . . . and . . . and, well I told Alan I wasn't going out in June after all. I couldn't go, so that was that.'

'Couldn't go? Why not?'

'What on earth's the point in asking me all these silly questions? I wasn't well! Anyway, I've told you already, I'd met Keith.'

'So you and Alan stopped writing to each other?'

'What was the point? I can't see why you want to know so much about him. I don't know what happened to him. I expect he married Sandra and they've half a dozen kids by now.'

If he doesn't change the subject soon I'll stop answering his questions, or tell him I've got a headache. He can't make me talk to him.

'So Keith took Alan's place? You liked him better than Charles?'

'I don't think "liking" came into it. Charles was very patient, very undemanding. Keith was the opposite. He wouldn't take "no" for an answer. Anyway, I didn't really want to say "no". Keith

146

and I . . . we were great together. That's when I moved in with him.'

'And Charles?'

'Oh, he was around. I saw him occasionally when I went home. I think my parents lived in hope that things would go wrong with Keith and I'd come to my senses and marry the faithful, eligible Charles.'

'You didn't think like that?'

'Maybe, from time to time. Charles wanted a family and I knew Keith didn't. I could see his point – he was trying to write and we only had the one room and not a penny between us. It was stupid of me really to think about it, but I envied Sue, my cousin. She'd been married three years and had two beautiful kids. She'd send me pictures.'

'It's natural to want children at your age.'

'I'd always planned on having a large family. Alan and I had decided to have at least six – three boys and three girls! Goes to show what silly ideas children can dream up. Who in their right mind would want to be saddled with a kid at my age – let alone six?'

'I think our time is up, Phillipa. I've enjoyed our talk. I won't be here at the clinic tomorrow, but I'll see you on Friday. Is that OK?'

'If you say so. You're the doctor – but I still think you're wasting your time. I'm feeling fine.'

'And looking better, too. I think we can safely reduce the number of pills you're taking. It should make you less sleepy.'

But I like sleeping. It stops me having to think.

147

'It's very good of you to come, Mrs McAlister. Did you have a good journey?'

Sue McAlister sat down in the armchair facing Phillipa's psychiatrist. She judged him to be in his fifties, an ordinary enough looking man but with a charming smile. Always quick to make judgements, she decided that she was going to like him. When she had spoken to him on the telephone from Toronto two days before, she had not been sure that she would.

'Phillipa has been doing everything she can to avoid me getting to the truth,' he had told her. 'She lies most convincingly, interlacing these fabrications with what I suspect is the truth. Her parents have thrown very little light on the matter. That's why I'm appealing to you. I think you may know her better than anyone. Would I be right?'

'Phillipa is one of the most honest people I've ever known!' Sue had replied. 'I can't imagine her lying!'

'She is very ill, Mrs McAlister. I'm the only person she talks to and if I lose this contact with her, she may stop communicating altogether. I should warn you, she may refuse to see you. So far she has reacted quite violently whenever a visitor has been mentioned . . . '

'The flight was fine, Dr Morton,' Sue replied now to his greeting. 'I'd have come sooner had I thought there was any way I could help. Her mother wrote and told me Pips had made a complete recovery from her fall and was recuperating in a nursing home; so until I had your call, I was unaware there'd been a set-back.'

'Can you tell me about Phillipa's wedding day? I've read the history, of course, but I'd like to hear what happened from you. You see, the curious thing about Phillipa's case is that she has, as her mother told you, made a complete physical recovery. It's her mental state that is causing concern. It's as if she became aware that she no longer had to face up to life whilst she was in that coma, and is now deliberately trying to recreate that brief spell of amnesia. All day long, she sits in a chair by the window, staring out into the garden, her eyes open but with what her nurses call a "trance-like" expression. Sometimes she weeps but doesn't seem aware she is crying. Other times, she smiles, but if her nurse asks her to share the joke, she pretends not to hear. Sometimes she holds that pink soft toy and rocks it as if it were a baby.'

'The rabbit is easily explained,' Sue said smiling. 'It always was the baby – I mean, when Pips and Alan and I used to play "fathers and mothers". Later, when she grew up, she kept it – the way some people keep their teddy bears.'

'So Phillipa is the maternal type. She tried on one occasion to infer the opposite.'

Sue frowned.

'I can't think why! It nearly broke her heart when Keith said he didn't want her to have the baby. Her letters were so depressed I'd have come over to comfort her if I hadn't been in the process of giving birth to my own child at the time. I suppose in a way that must have made the loss of her baby even more traumatic. You're looking surprised, Dr Morton. You did know about the abortion, didn't you?'

149

'No I didn't, although I half suspected something of the sort. Whose child was it?'

'Keith's of course. It was bad luck really! She'd only slept with him once. It was early on when she suspected Alan had fallen for that New Zealand girl. She wrote and told me about it. Keith was very attractive and he caught her at just the right moment.'

She gave a long sigh. 'The dreadful thing was, Alan still loved her. By the time she found that out, she'd discovered she was pregnant. Personally, I think she should have told Alan; but she didn't. She didn't tell anyone except Keith. To give Keith his due, he stood by her, but he certainly wasn't prepared to become a father. He talked her into having an abortion, arranged it all for her and paid for it. She was so worried by what her parents would say, she was tremendously grateful to him for covering it all up. I think it was partly gratitude which prompted her to move in with him. Needless to say, it didn't work out.'

Dr Morton nodded.

'So she didn't marry him – and there in the background was Charles. Yes, I see! So tell me about the accident. It happened on Phillipa's wedding day – or what should have been her wedding day. You were to have been her bridesmaid?'

'That's right! As a matter of fact, I was worried about Pips. She looked terribly pale and . . . sort of distraught. I thought she might have been having eleventh-hour jitters, and I told her she didn't have to go through with the wedding – that I'd get her out of it somehow. She said no, she was going to marry Charles – and I left.'

150

'What did you think about Phillipa marrying Charles? I met him briefly when he called to see her, and he seemed a very pleasant fellow. I believe he sends flowers every other day.'

Sue smiled.

'That's typical! He's terribly generous – and always does the right thing. He was very cut up when Phillipa was in hospital. I had a long talk with him in the visitors' room where we were both hoping to be able to see her. I think he half blamed himself . . . for the accident, I mean.'

'What possible reason did he have for that?'

As his visitor hesitated, Dr Morton added, 'Anything you tell me will be treated in absolute confidence, Mrs McAlister. Any facts you can give me, please do so. My task is not unlike that of a detective, you see. Any little thing may provide a clue!'

Sue nodded.

'I take your point, but I don't think this really does have any relevance. For what it may be worth, Charles had told Pips the night before the wedding that he'd been having an affair with Eva Astley-Grant. She was one of his girlfriends – a real Sloaney, green wellie brigade type, you know! Eva had been chasing him for years. I honestly don't know why he made this quite unnecessary confession; perhaps Pips asked him about her. But Pips wasn't the jealous type. She didn't like Eva – but who would! Very brittle, very county. She was also a bit of a bitch. She was always finding some way to bring the wretched Keith into the conversation, knowing full well that it upset Charles and embarrassed Pips.'

151

'Tell me more about Keith!'

'Where to begin? Devastatingly attractive; utterly self-centred; clever — his first book has been on all the bestseller lists. He knew just how to twist Pips round his little finger. He's quite a bit older than she is and to say he was a great deal more experienced is hugely understating the facts. He was quite clever, too, the way he seduced Pips. She was still in love with Alan when they met so she wasn't all that interested in him and I suppose that challenged him. Anyway, he took her to a dance, filled her up with champagne and took her back to his flat where the inevitable happened. Poor old Pips . . . she was horrified next day and resolved not to see him again — at least until she was more sure about Alan. The awful thing was, by the time Alan had caught up with her telephone messages and convinced her he still loved her and wanted to marry her, she'd discovered she was pregnant.'

'An unlucky twist of fate!' Dr Morton said.

'Yes, the timing couldn't have been worse. The trouble was, Pips sort of wanted to have the baby, but Keith certainly didn't want to marry her and there was no way she was going to tell Alan what had happened. Even after she'd had the abortion, she could have gone out to see Alan and he need never have known. But she wouldn't "cheat" — that's the way she put it in her letter. Anyway, Keith was hovering in the background — he really was crazy about her in those days. I think Pips thought Keith would help her get over Alan if she let him sleep with her. That part of the relationship was a success for a while, but sex was about all they did have in common.'

152

'What did Phillipa do with her time – after she'd had the abortion?'

'Nothing at first. She was very depressed. Eventually she took a dreary job in a travel agents to eke out their income – a total waste of her talents. Then she found out Keith had been having it off with another girl. She left him, but he persuaded her to go back. They had endless rows – usually because he was incapable of leaving other women alone. I think she left him three times before the final break. Even then, I think she might have gone back to him if it hadn't been for Charles.'

'How do you think the marriage to Charles would have worked out?'

Sue sighed.

'It's hard to say. I don't think Pips was in love with him. Come to that, I know she wasn't in love with Keith, either. I think she just wanted to get married and have children, and Charles was the obvious one for her to marry. At that point, she wrote and told me Keith had finally asked her to marry him. My guess is he knew he'd got to when he found out about her engagement to Charles. Poor old Pips seemed quite unable to make up her mind which of the two she wanted. I wrote back saying that if she wasn't sure, she shouldn't marry either! James, my husband, maintains that you shouldn't marry the man you must live with – only the one you can't live without – and I think he's right. I know I couldn't live without James. I've been so lucky!'

'So what would you advise Phillipa to do now – supposing she makes a complete recovery?'

'Make a new start, I suppose. I don't think

she should marry Charles or Keith. Perhaps she should go back to college, get her A levels and train to be a vet. That's what she and Alan both planned to do when we were kids. It was a pity that their Grand Plan came to nought. But who's to say Phillipa won't meet someone – at college perhaps? Nice as he was, Alan isn't the only man in the world who could share Pip's interests.'

'But she did love him. One last point Mrs McAlister. How did the final break with Alan come about?'

'Soon after Pips discovered she was pregnant. She wrote telling me that she knew Alan would never forgive her; that he deserved somebody "better", that he wouldn't understand how she could have wanted that baby even though it was another man's – and yet had allowed herself to be persuaded to "murder" it. She was riddled with guilt and frankly, one wonders how the doctor who counselled her at the time allowed the abortion to go ahead. I think she believed Alan would hate her – if he knew the truth – as much as she hated herself. She wrote and told him she'd found somebody else, and their engagement was off.'

Dr Morton nodded.

'Which explains why he never came back to England; why eventually he married the New Zealand girl.'

'I can't verify that. Alan never wrote to say he was getting married. All I know is that Pips believes he did. She wanted him to be happy, you see, and she felt so guilty about letting him down.'

There was a discreet knock on the door and one of the nurses came in with a tray.

'Sister thought you might like some tea, Mrs McAlister!' she said. She turned to the doctor and added, 'I'm afraid Phillipa has refused to see anyone. She became quite hysterical when we told her Mrs McAlister was here. Sister has given her a tranquillizer. We could try again in a little while.'

'No, don't force her!' Dr Morton said. 'I'm very sorry, Mrs McAlister, but perhaps tomorrow . . . or the next day? You're here for a week, aren't you? And please don't take this personally. I'm reasonably sure Phillipa's rejection of you is because you are the one nearest the truth she has been trying so hard to deny. Would it be too much to ask you to come and see me again tomorrow – about four-thirty? I'll have had another talk to Phillipa by then.'

'I've come all the way from Canada for one purpose only – to help my best friend get well. I'll be at your disposal, Doctor, any time, any day.'

As Sue stood up, so did the doctor.

'I think I may need your help,' he said, holding out his hand. 'You've been of great assistance already, but there is one thing I'd like you to do when you get back to your hotel.'

When five minutes later, Sue left the private clinic in Wimpole Street and hailed a taxi, unexpectedly empty in the rush hour traffic, she decided that her opinion of Dr Morton was a good one; and that if anyone could help Pips back to normality again, he would be the one.

155

'Sister said you didn't want to come and see me today, Phillipa. I'm sorry about that. I thought we were friends.'

He may have thought it – I didn't! I shan't answer any of his stupid questions. He can't make me.

'It wasn't very kind of you refusing to see your cousin yesterday. Mrs McAlister made a long and expensive journey for no other reason than to visit you.'

I don't want to see anyone. Certainly not Sue. Why can't they all leave me alone?

'Since you don't seem inclined to talk to me, it looks as if I will have to do the talking today. I'll tell you about the patient we admitted last night. She was a potential suicide . . . an old lady of sixty who had had to have her dog put to sleep. Very sad, but then life can be very sad. Hundreds of people try to end their lives in hundreds of different kinds of ways – and it's part of my job to make them come to terms with grief or guilt and learn to live again.'

That's hardly applicable to me. I didn't take an over-dose or . . .

'Some people think they can bury grief, simply by refusing to acknowledge it – the proverbial ostrich putting its head in the sand. But memories have a way of creeping out of crevices and catching you unawares – a song, perhaps, a smell, the sound of a voice. There isn't any permanent escape – though Old Father Time often helps. Death, of course, is one way, but mental death is, in its way, even worse. People have terrible car accidents and become what you call "vegetables". Others –

usually quite strong-willed – can induce this state simply by willing themselves into an imaginary world they like better than the real one. I've seen such cases – and I have to tell you that they are not usually happy people. It's as if they continue to fight the battles they were fighting in real life in their subconscious.'

If I close my eyes, he may think I've gone to sleep. I don't want to hear him droning on about his cases. Anyway, what I do with my life is my business, not his. I'm not listening to you, Dr Morton. I won't listen.

'I expect you read lots of fairy stories when you were a little girl, Phillipa. I'm going to tell you one now. It's about a little princess who met her prince when they were children. The prince knew of a beautiful castle on the far side of the forest where, when they found it, they could live. In time, he said, they would become king and queen and have little princes and princesses of their own, and live happily ever after. They set off together to search for the castle, but somehow they became separated and the princess lost her way . . . '

I don't like this story. I wish he'd stop talking. I won't listen, I won't!

'Of course, the story doesn't end there. The princess was so unhappy, she couldn't bear her sorrow. She went to see a wizard who could make spells. He gave her a magic potion which made her forget the prince, but only for a little while. She went to another wizard who offered her a beautiful castle, even bigger and nicer than the one her prince had described, and who promised to give her as many little princes and princesses as she wished if she would agree to marry him.

157

But he couldn't give her back her prince.'

'This is ridiculous nonsense! I'm not going to stay here and listen to you telling silly, childish stories. I don't like your posh clinic, or your nurses and most of all, I don't like you. I don't want to see you ever, ever again. Anyway, you don't know what you're talking about. She could have had her prince. I could have gone out to New Zealand after the abortion . . . I need never have told Alan . . . he needn't have known about the baby . . . I didn't have to tell him . . . '

'That's true! If you'd loved him less you could have deceived him,' Dr Morton said gently as the tears started rolling down her cheeks. 'But I think it would be a good idea, Phillipa, if you told me what you couldn't tell him.'

MONDAY

'May I introduce Alan Oakley, Dr Morton! We came straight here from Heathrow. It's good of you to fit us in to what I'm sure is a very busy schedule.'

'On the contrary, Mrs McAlister, I'm most grateful to you both for coming to see me.'

Dr Morton shook hands with Alan and invited them both to be seated.

'I was certainly not expecting to see you, Mr Oakley. When I asked Mrs McAlister to try and find out your telephone number in New Zealand, it was with the intention of asking you some questions over the phone.'

Alan nodded.

'So Sue explained! I had no idea Pips – Phillipa – had been so ill, or I'd have come back to England weeks ago. The last news I had was from her parents to say she was getting married. How is she? She is going to get well, isn't she?'

'I think I can reassure you on that point, Mr Oakley, although in this field, it is dangerous to make positive predictions. One is dealing with imponderables and it's only possible to make an educated guess as to what is going on in the subconscious. Obviously, the more familiar one is with the patient's life, character, upbringing and so on, the easier it is to see the wood for the trees. Or perhaps, in Phillipa's case, I should say: to see through the smoke screen she has chosen to put up. She is a lucky young lady, having friends prepared to fly to her assistance from all over the world!'

'The three of us – Sue, Pips and I – have known each other practically all our lives,' Alan said, running a hand through his hair. 'When Sue phoned me, I just dumped everything, packed an overnight bag and caught the next plane. I knew Pips must be pretty bad when Sue told me she had refused to see her. Although they're only cousins, they're closer than most sisters. Is Pips . . . is she very ill?'

'She has been – still is to some extent. I don't know how much Mrs McAlister has had time to tell you, but the problem really lies in the fact that Phillipa doesn't want to get well; to be obliged to take up the threads of her life again.'

'But I thought – surely if, when the accident happened, she was about to get married . . . ? I

159

mean, the fellow didn't back off at the last minute? He does still want to marry her?'

'It isn't Charles who's the problem, Alan,' Sue said. 'I'm pretty sure Pips never really wanted to marry Charles in the first place.'

'Then why . . . ?'

'Second best, perhaps! If she couldn't have the one man she did want . . . '

'Oh, you mean that chap she wrote and told me about!' Alan broke in. 'The one she met in London who wanted to write books.'

'No, not that one either, Alan. Keith was . . . '

Dr Morton had been listening in silence to this interchange. Now he said:

'Forgive me for interrupting you, Mrs McAlister, but there are one or two questions to which I need to know the answers before we discuss Phillipa any further. You are married, aren't you, Mr Oakley?'

'Great Scott, no! I'm what's known as a confirmed bachelor. Always will be, I dare say.'

'You mean you didn't marry Sandra?' Sue broke in.

Alan laughed.

'You have to be joking. Sandy's a dear – but hardly love's young dream. She must weigh all of sixteen stone – strong as a horse with muscles on her that put mine to shame. She can lift a fifty-six-pound sack of corn without turning a hair. Marvellous girl, though; rides like a cowboy, shears sheep like a pro; works as hard as any man. She wears breeches and swears with the best of the men around the place; and she can drink most of them under the table! I don't know where I would have been without her when I first went

160

out there. Sandy was the one who showed me the ropes, broke me in, you might say. As to marrying – I think there's only one man would dare take Sandy on – an Australian who comes over every year to help with the shearing.'

Dr Morton was smiling. Sue was looking surprised as she said falteringly:

'When you first went out to New Zealand, Sue told me your letters were mostly about this girl – how wonderful she was, how amusing, how kind, how well you got on together. Then there was the time Phillipa telephoned you and you and Sandra had gone off together skiing. It was then she assumed you'd found someone who meant more to you than she did.'

Alan looked bemused.

'But how could she? When I rang her back, I explained that neither Sandy nor I had had a break since her father died and I'd taken over the ranch, and we'd gone skiing with a party of her ex-schoolfriends. She had absolutely no cause to be jealous. Are you trying to tell me Pips thought I was in love with Sandy? I don't believe it!'

'*Until you rang her*, Phillipa did believe it. That's how she came to allow Keith into her life.'

Alan looked down at his hands, his eyes bitter.

'I was knocked sideways when she said she was postponing her visit. Then, later she wrote and told me she'd fallen for this guy and was living with him . . . Pips – my Phillipa! We'd made so many plans . . . promises . . . I couldn't believe she could just break it all up as if . . . as if I'd never really meant anything to her. I made an utter fool of myself – I was drunk for weeks. It was Sandy who

161

got me out of it; made me see that it was better for the break to happen before Pips came out to New Zealand and married me. The marriage wouldn't have worked, would it, if Pips had fallen out of love with me? I suppose finally, I did get over it – anyway, until I heard she was going to marry this Charles bloke. Then it hit me hard all over again. The truth is, daft as it sounds, I've never stopped loving her. I suppose I never will.'

Sue had fallen silent. Dr Morton's eyes were thoughtful. When he looked up, it was to say to Alan:

'I have little doubt that Phillipa has never stopped loving you. She broke off your engagement because of something she had done which convinced her she was unworthy of you.'

'I can't believe that. Pips was a wonderful person. She'd never deliberately do anything you could call "unforgivable", would she, Sue?'

'Perhaps she felt her options were limited,' Dr Morton interjected. 'The fact remains, she was not prepared to deceive you and she didn't believe you would forgive her if you knew the truth.'

Alan stood up, his expression defiant.

'Then she can't have known me as well as I thought she did. There is nothing I wouldn't have forgiven her. Surely if you really love someone, you don't reject them because of one transgression? I know Pips would never have deliberately done anything wrong. Whatever she did, it must have been by accident. See here, Dr Morton, I was in love with her, and I suppose I still am. I'd forgive her anything . . . anything at all. If she'd been unfaithful to me . . . been caught shoplifting . . .

162

killed someone . . . Can't you understand that?'

Dr Morton smiled.

'Indeed I can, Mr Oakley! Now suppose you go and see my patient? One of the nurses will show you her room – Number Twenty-two. I'll wait here and have a cup of tea with Mrs McAlister in case you need me. Somehow, I don't think you will.'

Alan did not return, but half an hour later, Gwen, the nurse, came in with a note.

'It's from Phillipa!' she said. 'It doesn't make much sense to me, Doctor, but she said it would to you.'

Dr Morton looked down at the scrap of paper on which was written:

> . . . and just when the princess thought she was lost forever, there on the edge of the forest was the prince, who all this time had been waiting for her. Like all good fairy tales, this one too, will end happily ever after. Thank you – from Phillipa.

'It's wonderful to see the two of them so happy, isn't it, Dr Morton?'

Sue smiled at the man standing by her side. A gentle breeze stirred the confetti surrounding the place where the bridal car had stood before driving the newly-weds to the airport. 'It was good of you to find time to come to the wedding!' she added. 'Pips was so anxious for you to be here. She and Alan both know they owe their happiness to you.'

'Perhaps! It depends, doesn't it? how romantically you view life. There are some who really believe that "true love will find a way"!'

Sue smiled.

'You surprise me, Dr Morton. I would have thought you'd seen enough tragedy in your job to be a total cynic. Tell me, when did you first realize Pips was still in love with Alan?'

'I don't know if I can answer that. It interested me that it was only when Phillipa started talking about her childhood with you and Alan, that she kept to the truth.'

'But why should she tell you all those untruths about Charles and Keith?'

'Because she couldn't bring herself to accept that life meant nothing to her if she couldn't have Alan. I don't doubt she had imagined what marriage to Charles and Keith would be like; tried on many occasions to convince herself that one or the other could work out.'

'You don't think . . . that awful day when she fell downstairs . . . you don't think she did so deliberately?'

'Not for one moment! She was simply not concentrating. After all, you had offered her a get-out if she'd not wanted to go through with the marriage to Charles.'

They began to walk slowly up to the house where Phillipa's mother was now serving tea.

'At least poor old Charles hasn't had his heart broken!' Sue said laughing. 'I saw an announcement of his engagement to Eva Astley-Grant in the *Telegraph* this morning. He didn't waste much time!'

'Probably he got the message when Phillipa steadfastly refused to see him all those weeks she was ill.'

164

'Eva is just the right kind of wife Charles needs –
the ideal society hostess!' Sue smiled. 'As for Keith
– Pips says he's in the States on a publicity tour,
promoting his new book. Doubtless the American
women are lionizing him – he's so good-looking!'

'And what about you, Mrs McAlister?'

'I go back home tomorrow. I'm lucky, aren't I,
to be married to such an understanding husband.
James said I could stay as long as I was needed,
and that included being Pips' matron-of-honour
today. We'd always promised each other we'd
never marry unless the other was an attendant.'

'So Phillipa told me. Now I must be getting back
to town!' Dr Morton said. 'I'll go and pay my re-
spects to our host and hostess. I expect they'll be
glad to see the back of me.'

Sue laughed.

'I think you're forgiven, Dr Morton. One can't
blame them for hating the thought of Pips going
to live in New Zealand, but they're much more concerned about her getting well again. I know they're
very grateful.' She paused in the doorway. 'Before
we say goodbye, will you answer one last question?
Why did you want me to telephone Alan? What
were you hoping to find out?'

Dr Morton shrugged.

'The truth, I think. Phillipa had told me so many
untruths about Keith and Charles, I couldn't be
sure whether or not she was still in love with Alan,
or, indeed, if he'd ever married. I'd realized, looking at my notes, that Phillipa had never stated it as
a fact – only as a supposition. She was so certain of
it, she half convinced me; but I needed to be sure.
I suppose to some extent, it was a shot in the dark.

It was a real bonus when instead of a phone call, Alan himself turned up. Not all my cases are so easily – or so happily – resolved, believe me. One has failures as well as successes, although we don't talk about them!'

Sue nodded.

'There must be times when you get pretty depressed yourself, Dr Morton!'

The psychiatrist laughed.

'Indeed there are, Mrs McAlister! Unlike surgeons who can see the damage they have to rectify, we, to a large extent, are feeling around in the dark. Sometimes, when I can't help a patient, I wonder if I wouldn't be more useful doing some other, easier job. The temptation is there.'

'But you don't give in to it?'

'No, I have a remedy. I look through the list of my successes. I can add another one to that list now.'

'Phillipa!' said Sue, with a long sigh of satisfaction.

'Yes, indeed,' agreed Dr Morton with a smile, 'the patient who tried to lock herself away from life in Number Twenty-two.'

Comfort and Joy

'Can I have another banana?'

'No!'

'Why can't I? You said fruit was good for me.'

'Because we're snowed in and I'll have to walk two miles in deep snow to get every bit of food you eat, so everything is rationed.'

'What's rationed mean?'

'Go and do some tobogganing!' Janie suggested a little too quietly. Edward, her six-year-old son, sensed her exasperation and beat a hasty retreat.

He's too young to realize how worried I am, Janie thought, a sense of guilt now momentarily overriding the anxiety which had dogged her ever since Hugo had determined to try to get to work that morning.

'Yesterday was the coldest day in Britain since 1895,' the man on the radio had announced cheerfully on the eight o'clock news. He had followed up this piece of information with lurid descriptions of the number of road accidents there had been; the burden on the hospitals' casualty staff; the growing disruption to road, rail and air transport and regional failures of electricity and telephone supplies.

The lunchtime weather forecast was little better, despite the optimistic tone of the announcer's voice when he detailed what was obvious to anyone looking out of their window that morning – the Big Freeze of the winter of 1956 was over and very heavy snowfalls had been reported all over the country.

'Darling, I haven't been able to get up to the office for two days!' Hugo had endeavoured to explain his determination to get to work even if he 'died in the attempt!' She had managed a smile which was quickly wiped off her face when she listened to the lunchtime reports of a *'terrible rail crash'* south of London. If anything happened to Hugo . . .

With an effort Janie curbed her imagination. She spent the next half-hour trying to make a cake with porridge oats, her supply of flour having run dangerously low. The mixture looked so unappetizing, she threw it out for the birds. Sighing, she realized it meant she could not postpone much longer the two-mile trek with the sledge to the village. Hugo had failed yet again to get the car up the drive and had had to put on his wellies and trudge through the snow in the hope of catching a bus to the station. She would have to do the same. She must also get at least two days supply of milk to drag down. Ten pints in a crate . . . how many pounds, she wondered, in ten pints?

'Mum!'

'What's the matter now?'

'I've got hiccups. They keep interrupting me.'

Janie abandoned her calculations.

'Well, *you* keep interrupting *me!*' she said, giving him a glass of water since there was no milk.

'Tony's fallen over and cut his face!' Edward reported as an afterthought. 'There's ever such a lot of bright red blood. Will he have to go to hospital?'

170

'He can't!' Janie was almost shouting. 'We're *cut off*!'

Hurriedly she donned her wellies and anorak to rush off to the rescue of their visitor. Ploughing through the snow towards the field, she tried not to imagine what Tony's mother would say when he was returned to her with a broken bone – or at best covered in cuts. Maybe, she thought, she should not have allowed the children to use the toboggan unsupervised . . .

'You've gone green!' Edward said as they plodded into the field and she could now see the figure of her eldest daughter, Kelly, bent over the prone figure of their guest.

'Kelly says blue and yellow make green in my paint box. If you mixed red blood and . . . '

'Be quiet!' Janie ordered. 'You'll get hiccups again.'

Kelly looked up as they approached. She said comfortingly, 'It's mostly a nosebleed, Mummy.'

Later, as Janie bathed and disinfected Tony's cuts, she wondered if it was possible for scabs to form and disappear in two days – before their visitor went home.

'I s'pect you'll have those scars for life!' Edward informed his friend with relish. 'Can I have an apple, Mum?'

Six years ago, almost to the day, Janie thought, she had given birth to her son. Great Aunt Edith, who professed to have second sight, had solemnly declared that this child would, as he grew older, prove to be 'an enduring comfort and joy' to her in times of trouble. Clearly, he wasn't old enough yet!

171

'Was war like this?' asked Kelly. 'I mean the rationing?'

'No! You've had more butter on those last two pieces of bread than we had to last a week.'

'Is that why you're so thin?' asked Edward.

'No! I'm thin because I'm a worrier.'

He frowned. 'You said there wasn't anything to worry about. You said as long as we had the toboggan, we could get food. You said it wouldn't go on snowing for ever. Probably by next summer, it'll have stopped. Could you have two bananas in the war?'

'There's eighty-two of us at our boarding school!' said Tony. 'I wonder how they'd get enough food for all of us if it wasn't the holidays.'

'It's still snowing!' said Edward, gazing out of the window. 'I don't suppose Daddy will ever get home tonight. I expect his train will get buried in a snow drift and he'll probably be dead. What's it like being dead, Mum?'

'Go and watch TV,' Janie said.

SUPPER TIME

'Can't I have three sausages?'

'No! Two each.'

'It's still snowing. I wonder if Daddy ever got to the station this morning. It said on TV just now that the roads have got snow on top of black ice. How can ice be black, Mum?'

'This cocoa tastes funny!' said Kelly.

172

'I'm sorry, dear, it's tinned milk. There's no fresh milk left.'

'What'll we have for lunch tomorrow?'

'Could I have a piece of plaster for my toe?'

'Oh, Tony, what have you done now?' Janie cried, lifting her youngest child, Amy, down from the table.

'I just tore a bit of toe-nail off by mistake. It'll be all right.'

Janie hoped his mother would think so.

'Of course, if the snow gets much deeper, Tony won't be able to go home for ages and ages,' Edward said happily.

'Have you fed the rabbits?' Janie suggested as she dealt with Tony's foot.

'We can't!' said the children, adding in unison, 'There's no food!'

'Will they starve, Mum, if we can't feed them?' Edward asked. 'Will they get thinner and thinner until they turn into skeletons and . . . ?'

'Eat up your bread and butter!' Janie ordered as she dished up Tony's sausages.

'I can't!' Edward said with a sigh. 'I just can't!'

'Why not? I thought you were hungry after all that tobogganing.'

'I'm too 'zorsted to be hungry.'

'You need to eat in this cold weather.'

'Then why haven't you eaten yours?'

Janie, too, was exhausted.

'Can I have some jelly?'

'But you said just now you were too tired to eat.'

'Well, I've rested since then. Can I?'

'Isn't it time for the news?' said Kelly. 'There might be another weather forecast!'

173

Janie switched on the radio.

'*There will be more snow all over the country during the night with particularly heavy falls in the south in Kent, Sussex and . . .* '

'Why, that's us!' shouted Edward. 'Did you hear the man saying about us, Mum?'

'Off you go and play!' Janie said. 'Half an hour – and then it's bedtime.'

'But we can't go out *now*,' said Edward. 'It's still snowing!'

BEDTIME

'Where's Tony?'

'He's lying down. He's got a pain!'

'It's probably just indigestion!' said Kelly. 'He's been eating acid drops.'

'If you get a pain on the right side of your tummy, it's a 'pendicitis!' said Edward. 'I saw it on telly.'

Tony appeared in the doorway.

'I'm feeling better now,' he said. 'I think the pain was just wind.'

'Daddy said if we have much wind today, it'll probably make deep drifts up by the Jacksons. If they get as deep as Daddy, would he be able to walk through them?'

Kelly said thoughtfully, 'If Daddy doesn't get home by nine, how would you know if it was just because the trains were late again or if he was stuck in a snow drift?'

'We could go and dig him out,' Edward suggested.

174

'We could do it by torchlight. We can use the gun torch I got for Christmas. Would he be frozen stiff like a board or could he walk when we'd dug him out?'

'Silly!' said Tony scornfully. 'It'd depend how long he'd been there. If he'd been there for hours and hours, he'd probably be dead.'

'If he does die and you die, too, Mum, can I have your electric blanket?'

'If someone did die, how would you bury them with all that snow?' asked Kelly.

'Yes, how would you?' said Edward, warming to the subject. 'If you just dug a hole in the snow, when it melted, there'd be a corpse and . . . '

'Go away! Go away!' Janie said desperately. 'You've ten more minutes before it's time for your baths. Go and play ping-pong, Cluedo, Snap – murder if you like.'

The back door opened and Hugo came into the kitchen. His hair was covered by snow flakes; his raincoat and wellies dripped water on to the tiled floor. Kelly flung herself into his arms, hugging him. Edward clung to his arm.

'We've had a smashing day, Dad,' he said.

'Been looking after Mum for me, have you?' Hugo said, smiling at Janie over the children's heads. 'Been a great comfort to her, I hope?'

' 'Course we have!' Edward answered. 'We went tobogganing and Tony fell off and he was covered in blood and after that we pretended we were lost in a drift and Kelly was Mum looking for you and I was you and she couldn't find me because I was buried up to my neck in snow and I was dead!'

175

'I see Great Aunt Edith's prophecy has come to pass!' Hugo said pointedly.

Perhaps it had, Janie thought, realizing that for the first time that day, Edward had finally made her laugh.

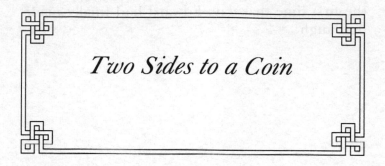

Two Sides to a Coin

I cannot remember how I felt about my Uncle Bob before the age of six, although Mother and I visited my aunt and uncle regularly four times a year. They lived in Eastbourne in a neat little bungalow in a street leading off the promenade. I do remember that I enjoyed going there because it meant a ride in a bus to Victoria Station from our tiny maisonette in north London followed by a train ride. As Mother had been widowed in 1917, we had very little money and such treats were rare. However, I did not like being there. I suppose I sensed my Aunt Ruby's disapproval of children; and Mother's insistence that I should be on my very best behaviour added to my anxiety.

Aunt Ruby was Mother's sister. She was not in the least like Mother who was thin and even in those days when she must have been quite young, going grey. My aunt was plump with rosy cheeks framed by thick, carefully waved hair. I disliked her for several reasons; not only because I knew she was disinterested in me, but also because she criticized my mother who I adored. In those very early years, Mother always took with us a jigsaw or a book to crayon and I would be told to amuse myself whilst Mother and Aunt Ruby 'had a quiet chat' in the sitting-room. Uncle Bob would be detailed to sit in the dining-room with me to see that I didn't get up to mischief. Most of the time, he read his newspaper but occasionally, I would find him looking over my shoulder and with his quiet, rather shy smile, he would add a missing piece to my jigsaw or draw a funny face in my colouring book.

By the age of seven, my feelings towards my uncle became more definite. Had I possessed the ability to define them, I would have described them as a mixture of sympathy and irritation; towards my aunt, an acute antipathy.

'She's so bossy!' I complained inadequately to my mother. I expected Aunt Ruby to tell me to 'sit up straight, Robert!' 'Don't touch that, you might break it!' 'You can go for a walk but be back by four for tea!' But it did not seem right to me that she should dictate to my uncle as if he, too, were a child. He would never argue with her but nod his head and say, 'Yes, dear!' no matter what she told him to do – or not to do. She even made him eat what she considered 'suitable foods' and would not permit him to have what he preferred.

'Your aunt is devoted to Uncle Bob!' Mother endeavoured to explain, 'and her big fear is that he might die before her. That's why she fusses about his diet.'

By the age of eleven, I knew that fat people often died from heart attacks but it was Aunt Ruby who was over-weight – not skinny little Uncle Bob.

'He only has porridge for breakfast!' I protested. 'He said I was a lucky boy to have scrambled egg or bacon, and he wished he could have the same. She makes him have what *she* wants!'

'Only for his own good, dear!' Mother insisted, 'and don't say "she"!'

To say that at this stage of my life I despised him

180

for giving in to Aunt Ruby would not be entirely untrue, yet I was confused by the fact that I liked being with him. He seldom spoke, even when we were alone on one of our interminable walks along the prom; but it was he who made those long afternoons whilst Mother and Aunt Ruby chatted, not only tolerable but enjoyable. He would stop by the telescope and continue to put money in the slot so that I could watch the boats or search for the French coast for as long as I wanted. He bought candy-floss and home-made fudge, all of which we consumed without one admonition that it would 'spoil our appetites'. When it rained and Aunt Ruby would not allow us to go out lest we caught cold, we played cards and chess and backgammon. I don't recall that he ever suggested we should keep secret the fact that we played for money – real money – but it was never mentioned when we were made to stop for tea. I think Mother must have guessed because she couldn't afford on her meagre widow's pension to give me much pocket money and yet she never asked me about the half crowns or ten bob notes I produced after one of our visits.

Aunt Ruby did not approve of my going to a fee paying school; she thought it extremely silly of my mother to take in sewing in order to be able to afford my uniform. My fees, fortunately, were covered by the scholarship I'd won so she couldn't say anything about that! I never knew what Uncle Bob thought about it since he never expressed an opinion if it were contrary to that of my aunt.

By the time I was fifteen, I was less critical of

181

Uncle Bob's inability to stand up for himself for I had begun to realize that he was a painfully shy, reserved man and I myself was going through the adolescent stage of acute self-consciousness. An inability to express one's deepest emotions was not after all a matter of being inarticulate so much as choosing not to reveal one's vulnerability. Now, at Christmas, Easter and on my birthday, I would receive a banknote in an envelope from Uncle Bob as well as the rather boring present sent from both of my relations and clearly chosen by Aunt Ruby since it was, without fail, something 'useful' – a scarf or tie or gloves – which I never wore. Uncle Bob's cash donations were very welcome. They always arrived with a note saying 'Expect you can make use of this – no need to write.' I took this to mean he did not wish to be embarrassed by my thanks, although it did occur to me that Aunt Ruby might not have been asked if she approved of the gift and must not, therefore, be made aware of it.

Mother no longer insisted that I accompany her on her visits to Eastbourne, although when I protested my unwillingness to do so on the grounds that neither my aunt nor my uncle really wanted to see me, she led me to understand that my presence was necessary to everyone's enjoyment of the day – I could be paired off with Uncle Bob, thus leaving Mother and Aunt Ruby to enjoy their talks in private.

At sixteen, I stopped growing and Mother no longer had to pay out unwelcome sums for new uniform. She saved the money instead for a summer holiday and booked us into bed-and-breakfast accommodation in Newquay. It was the first holiday we'd ever had, discounting the day trips to Eastbourne. Unfortunately, shortly before we were due to go, Mother developed an appendicitis, which required immediate hospitalization. She could see that I was unable to disguise my horror at her suggestion that I spend the week in Eastbourne where I could be looked after by Aunt Ruby. She was also worried about the waste of money since she had had to pay our landlady in advance. I did not know whether to be relieved or dismayed when, following a telephone call to Aunt Ruby, I was told that Uncle Bob would go to Newquay in Mother's place.

I have had many holidays in my latter years, some to exotic places like Bali and Bermuda and India but none that, in retrospect, I enjoyed as much as I did that strange holiday with my uncle. He treated me as if I were really grown-up; took me to my first pub; to Land's End; to Bedruthen Steps and to Padstow. We went mackerel fishing, mini golfing, to the cinema, to a variety show. We walked for miles on the sands and the cliffs, not saying much, of course, but mutually enjoying the sun, the salt smell of the sea, the feeling of freedom. We ate enormous breakfasts and bought fish and chips or whelks and ice cream for lunches. I thought about Aunt Ruby's diets and, having a morbid imagination at that stage of my adolescence, wondered how I would break the news to her if my uncle were to die from the expected heart attack which she so feared.

I don't think that I had ever heard my uncle say one unkind word about Aunt Ruby although, with the years, she had become steadily more

183

dictatorial and even my mother admitted that poor Uncle Bob was the proverbial hen-pecked husband. However, on the train taking us back to London from Newquay, my uncle, who had been staring out of the window for some time, suddenly said, 'I wish we could have had another week!' His tone was so wistful that for one terrible moment, I thought he was going to weep. I longed to be able to tell him that I, almost a man myself, understood how unhappy and humiliated he must feel living with such a wife; that if I had been he, I would have left her years ago!

As he saw me on to the bus with my suitcase, he slipped a fiver into my hand – the first I'd ever had.

'Buy your mother something nice!' he said, adding as always, 'No need to write and thank me.'

Nevertheless, Mother insisted upon writing and I had a job to persuade her to give the letter to me to post. I put it in the waste bin by the bus stop. Somehow I knew Aunt Ruby mustn't find out that my uncle had given away some money without her say-so. There were times like that when I wished she were dead.

It came, therefore, as a very unpleasant shock when two weeks later, Mother received a telegram from Uncle Bob saying that Aunt Ruby was indeed dead. She had had a massive coronary and had died before the ambulance came. I felt miserably guilty on two counts – one that I had wished this misfortune on her and the other that I wasn't the least bit sorry she'd gone.

'Goodness only knows how your poor Uncle Bob

184

will manage without her!' Mother said, so for his
sake I did regret her death.

Mother was still convalescing and couldn't go
to the funeral. I went instead. I spent the day
listening to distant relatives, close neighbours and
friends asking each other how ever poor Uncle
Bob would survive without Aunt Ruby to look
after him. He certainly looked forlorn – but
then he usually did. After all the visitors had
left, he cheered up a bit and took me on a tour
of the house.

'Your aunt never made a will, believing I'd go
before her, else I'm sure she'd have left you something,' he said. 'Say if there's anything you fancy,
my boy.' It was one of those rare occasions in my
life that I saw him smile. 'Don't suppose there's
much to your taste – but this might be useful.'

He pointed to an old wall-bracket clock which
had fascinated me ever since I could remember.
It had a delightful chime which peeled even the
quarter hours.

'Your aunt didn't much care for it – it was my
grandmother's, so it may be worth a bob or two
one day. You take it, Robert.'

We didn't see Uncle Bob again. I went back to
school and the following Christmas holidays, we
went to stay with a cousin of Mother's in Wales.
Mother didn't care to talk about Aunt Ruby whose
death she had felt very keenly, Aunt Ruby being
her only sister. She never talked about Uncle Bob
although we all exchanged Christmas cards and
I always received a birthday card with a cheque
enclosed. I wrote to him from time to time when
I was at university, and I meant to go and see

185

him, although by then I had a great many friends of my own age and I never seemed to have time to spare. I wrote, with youthful self-centredness about myself, and he wrote back about my affairs, never about himself. I thought about him sometimes when I was at home and heard the clock chime, but mostly I never thought about him at all.

Soon after leaving university, I got a good job in Scotland and married an Edinburgh girl. Mother lived with us during the Second World War, and helped my wife when the children came along. We didn't have much money but then I'd never been used to it and my wife was a wonderful cook and housekeeper. We were very happy. Unlike Aunt Ruby, my wife was more than content to let me be 'the man of the house'.

By the time my children were grown-up, Uncle Bob was in his eighties and we were in the process of planning a holiday in England to include a visit to Eastbourne, when I received a letter from a Mrs Catherine Buckly telling me that my uncle had died. Despite the intermittence of our relationship, I was surprisingly distressed. I decided to go to the funeral. Mother had died the previous year and my wife did not know Uncle Bob, so I went on my own. It was a cold, blustery day in Eastbourne and as my taxi drove me along the seafront, waves were pounding in over the pebbles and I thought, nostalgically, of my uncle allowing me to approach such waves and dart away as they came rushing in; how inevitably, I left it too late and got my boots and socks soaked; how we'd sat by a radiator in a nearby café and tried to dry them out before facing

186

Aunt Ruby's wrath. I realized then that I'd really loved my uncle; that he'd been very good to me in a quiet, unobtrusive way.

There were only three people other than the undertakers, the vicar and the gravedigger at the funeral. I was one of the three mourners, Uncle Bob's lawyer was the second and Mrs Catherine Buckly the third. She was a tiny, bird-like woman, very frail and elderly, and throughout the service she leant on my arm. I assumed she was a relative of my uncle's since she had his surname. She seemed to take it for granted that I would go back to the house afterwards. It was only then that I learned this old lady was Uncle Bob's second wife. He'd never told me he had remarried.

'You feature in the will,' the lawyer explained to me when we were settled in the dining-room where once Uncle Bob had helped me with my jigsaws, and lost to me – on purpose, I had long since realized – at poker. 'I don't think there is any need for me to read it formally. Mrs Buckly inherits the bulk of your uncle's not inconsiderable estate. You are the only other beneficiary, to the tune of ten thousand pounds!'

My astonishment was total. Why me? I had not seen my uncle for over thirty years.

After the lawyer had left, Mrs Buckly invited me to seat myself in what had been Uncle Bob's chair. Having placed a large whisky and soda in my hand, she sat down opposite me.

'Forgive me if I call you by your Christian name,' she said. 'You see, I feel I know you very well. Your uncle has talked to me about you since the day you were born.'

187

Gradually, the story she had to tell me unfolded. She had been a typist in the solicitor's office where Uncle Bob, as a young man, had been employed before the First World War. She had fallen in love with him but he had met and married my Aunt Ruby, at that time a very pretty young girl. Soon after the marriage, Aunt Ruby became pregnant and Uncle Bob, knowing nothing of his typist's secret feelings for him, confided in her how delighted he was by his approaching fatherhood. During his years in the trenches in France, he had thought of little else but how sad it would be to die without leaving a trace of himself behind.

'His joy was short-lived,' Mrs Buckly explained. 'The baby – a boy – was premature and in those days, there were not the modern facilities for saving its life.'

Aunt Ruby became severely depressed and spent some months in a psychiatric hospital. When she came out, she and Uncle Bob learned that there could never be any more children. Thereafter, Uncle Bob became Aunt Ruby's child, she his mother. The marriage, as such, continued but not as a marriage should be. Aunt Ruby's devotion was that of a mother only. She became obsessed with the fear that Uncle Bob might die as her child had done, prematurely, and leave her on her own.

'So you see, Robert, your uncle had little choice but to play the part of the child. He had come to know of my affection for him and, after I had become his personal secretary, he acknowledged his love for me. We both knew how dependent your aunt was upon him and that as long as she lived, we could never declare ourselves. We took lunch together every day and when we were younger, we would use the lunch hour to walk, taking a sandwich with us. We did not even hold hands.'

Seeing my expression, she smiled.

'You must remember, Robert, we were a different generation. Duty, divorce, illicit liaisons – they had very different values in those days. I never married, which worried your uncle – but then I had no wish to share my life with anyone else. I was fifty when your aunt died. Your uncle said we had wasted enough of our lives and we should not waste further precious days. We were married secretly a fortnight after your aunt's death. Only your mother was told – and quite naturally, she was deeply shocked, believing that we should have had more respect for her sister's memory. I moved into this house with your uncle and we have had thirty-five very happy years. I do not regret one minute of them. I loved him dearly!'

I was in no doubt about it and could understand now why he had left this elderly lady most of his worldly goods. But there was still one more question needing an answer.

'Why me?' I asked. 'I hardly knew him!'

'But he knew you – and loved you very much,' Mrs Buckly said. '*He* had become your aunt's "child", replacing her lost baby; but *you* were his "son". You were born the same year, you know. Your mother sent him a photograph of you which he brought to the office and showed me.

' "Our son, too, was fair haired, blue-eyed. This child could have been ours!" he said.'

Perhaps for that very reason, Mrs Buckly continued, Aunt Ruby could not bear to have me

189

around, but since there was no one else but my mother to take care of me, my aunt had had to endure my presence in those childhood years. Each time my poor Aunt Ruby had seen me, she had been forced once more to remember her loss. I understood now why she could not help disliking me.

So finally, I also understood how badly I had misjudged the relationship between my uncle and aunt, believing her to be the bully, he the weak one. I wished – and still do – that my mother was alive so that I could ask her why she never explained all this to me. Perhaps she thought at first that I was too young to understand, and then, by the time I was adult, that it wasn't any of my business. I'll never know. All I can be sure of is that I loved my uncle much more than I realized as a child, and that he had loved me.

'You were one of the few real joys in his life,' Mrs Buckly said as I left. ' "A fine boy, young Robert!" he used to say, "Just the sort of son I'd have liked." '

I have tried to recall the quiet, hen-pecked little man I had once, in the folly of my youth, despised for his weakness of character but I can no longer do so. I think of him now as a strong man with a very big heart and a stature that I am trying to emulate. I suppose at this late stage of my life, I try to model myself on him as I might have done my father. I no longer judge anyone on outward appearances for I have learned that there are two sides to every coin.

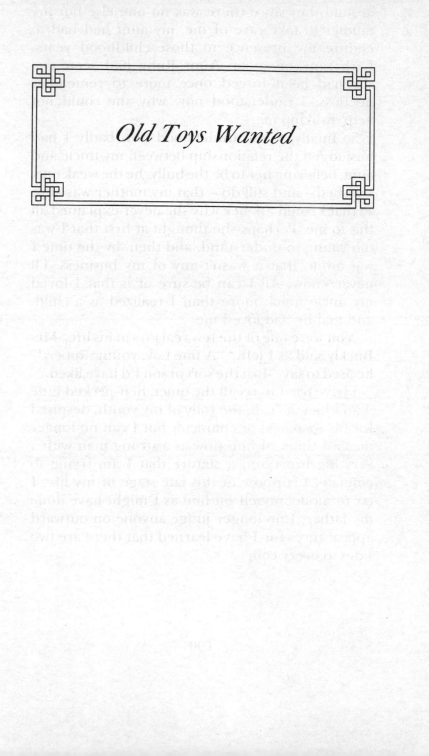

Old Toys Wanted

I've had some strange jobs to do in my life as a removal man. Met some strange people; some nice, some I'd not want to meet again. But since you're asking me which job sticks most in the memory, I suppose it has to be packing up the toys in Thomas P. Culpepper's shop. In a village near Marlborough, it was — one of those sleepy little villages with quaint old buildings and shops. Mr Culpepper's shop was a little bit of a place; might have come out of a book by Dickens — just the one, square-paned, bow window with that funny bobbly glass.

We'd been told by our boss to go down and pack everything up, label the crates and bring them back to the warehouse 'cos the new owner wanted them stored till Christmas. Bill and me were busy wrapping and packing all these toys — antique, they were, out of the ark — but some of 'em was fascinating. Bill was showing me how one of them clockwork money-boxes worked when in walked this lady. Very elegant, she was, and rich, too. Had one of those big Daimler cars outside with a chauffeur in the front to drive her.

'Excuse me,' she says, 'but do you know what happened to the teddy bear — the scruffy old one in the window?'

Bill said as how he'd already packed it but she offered us five quid each if we'd find it for her; said it was hers and she'd pay the 4/6d it was marked up at so as no one would be the worse off. Well, we weren't going to argue — not with five quid in the offing, so we found it for her.

She was that pleased when we came on that moth-eaten old thing! Naturally, Bill and me was dead curious and

193

when we told her we'd no idea who had owned the shop, coming from London like, she offered to tell us about Thomas P. Culpepper. She'd been five years old when she first came to live in that village. Her ma had died not long since and her pa had come to work in the neighbourhood. They were quite poor and since her dad couldn't afford a governess nor housekeeper to look after her, her aunt had taken on the task. Her aunt hadn't liked children . . . but that's running away with the story. I'll try to tell it much as she told it to us. It began in the spring of 1902.

It was not unusual for children walking home from the church school further down the road to stop and look in Mr Culpepper's window, but they seldom lingered long. Freed from the restrictions of the classroom, they chattered and fidgeted and laughed as they glanced briefly at the toys before hurrying away to their families for tea and playtime. All the toys in his shop were too old to interest these children who spent their pocket money on shiny modern playthings made in factories.

One child, however, did linger, flattening her snub nose against the dusty squares of glass. Since it was early summer, she shaded her eyes against the sun's reflection in the high bay window, the better to see the toys on display.

He noticed her particularly, partly because she was always by herself, partly because her panama hat was several sizes too large; the white elastic which should have attached it to her head, looped beneath her chin. The height of his bay window prohibited any view of her body and legs but he knew she was small and thin.

194

The term was almost over before one hot, dusty day, she edged through the doorway into Mr Culpepper's cool, shadowy shop. Her movements were so hesitant, Mr Culpepper decided it might be best not to speak. He continued dusting the bars of the singing canary's gold cage, his green eye-shade almost touching his pince-nez and keeping the few remaining strands of wispy white hair off his forehead.

Presently, the child asked, 'Does it sing?'

Mr Culpepper nodded, glancing briefly at the pale face and noting the freckles bridging the snub nose. She was not a pretty child, except for her eyes which were blue – a deep, moist, violet blue.

'Oh, yes, it sings!' he said. 'If you've got a moment to spare, I'll wind it up for you and you can hear it.'

He wound up the mechanical singing bird and as he stood there listening, his duster in one hand, the key in the other, the rapture on his deeply wrinkled face was no less than that on the face of the child. The sweet clear notes of the canary's song filled the dark, dusty interior of the shop with joy.

'One day, if I'm ever rich enough, I'll buy it – that is, if you haven't sold it by the time I'm grown-up. I'm six now, so it could be quite a long time . . .'

Her voice trailed away uncertainly.

'I made up my mind to buy one just like it when I was about your age,' Mr Culpepper said, resuming his dusting. 'This one is over a hundred years old. The poor little bird has lost a few feathers, I'm afraid, but it sings as well as it ever could have done, don't you think?'

As the child nodded, her panama hat slipped forward over her nose and with a sigh, she removed it.

'I should go home to tea now,' she said, but she remained where she was, her eyes wide as she looked at the crowded shelves and table tops. There were china dolls in a variety of costumes and a tin-plated miniature donkey and cart which had once moved, Mr Culpepper told her, but he had lost the key. There was a magical carousel with papier-mâché horses which Mr Culpepper turned with a wooden handle. On a shelf by themselves were a number of engines with brightly painted carriages but these, the old man informed his fascinated visitor, were only a little older than she was, because trains hadn't been invented very long before she was born. The doll's houses, rocking horses and model ships were early nineteenth century, made when the late Queen Victoria was only a little girl, he elaborated.

From one of the dark corners of the shop, an old clock chimed the hour. The child's face, which had rounded with pleasure at this Aladdin's cave, counted the time.

'I've got to go now. Aunt Hilda will be cross if I'm late for tea.'

It was several days before Mr Culpepper saw her again. He supposed that like the other children, she had been taken to the seaside for the hot month of August; or else was picnicking in the woods or picking buttercups in the green meadows. It was quiet in the High Street in summer, although sometimes a motor car would stop and a passing visitor would come into his shop to buy something. They always left empty-handed.

She came into the shop a third time less cautiously, a battered teddy bear tucked under her arm. The school uniform had been replaced by a check gingham dress which, like her school clothes, was two sizes too large for her.

'I didn't know what to do so I thought I'd come and see you,' she said when she had mustered up courage to talk to Mr Culpepper's back. He was bent over a shiny brass engine, upturned whilst he oiled its works with a tiny oil can. She watched as the golden liquid droplets fell one by one on to the delicate mechanism.

'I wish I could oil the engines, but I expect I'd spill it. I'm always spilling things. Aunt Hilda says I was born clumsy!'

As Mr Culpepper put away the oil can and replaced the engine on its shelf, he said comfortingly, 'It's only because your hands are so small. But small hands can be very useful – for getting inside things.' He walked over to a drawer and after rummaging about in it for a few minutes, took out a cast iron money-box. The figure of a monkey with hand outstretched to receive a coin was perched on top.

'He's supposed to put the coin in his mouth and the mechanism makes him toss up his hand, so the coin slips in,' explained Mr Culpepper. 'But I'm afraid someone must have fed him a bent penny. Perhaps with your little hands, you could manage to unjam it for me?'

197

'Aunt Hilda says I'm not usually very good at doing things,' she muttered doubtfully. But she managed to retrieve the coin with an ease which clearly surprised her.

'There now! Let's see if it works,' said Mr Culpepper approvingly. He watched the delight fill her face as she stared at the monkey tossing each coin she gave it with mechanical obedience.

'That's good!' he said. 'You've made it work again.'

So began a friendship which lasted through August and into September. Every day, when she came to Mr Culpepper's shop, he found her little tasks to perform. She worked happily, and for the most part, silently. But sometimes, she asked questions.

'Nobody ever buys anything from your shop, do they, Mr Culpepper?'

'I dare say not!'

'But it says: OLD TOYS WANTED, BOUGHT AND *SOLD*.'

'Well, I do buy sometimes if I see something I fancy, but selling – well, that's another matter.'

An hour later, she said, 'I don't think you want to sell your toys, Mr Culpepper. It's because you love them all too much.'

'Now what makes you think that?' Mr Culpepper prevaricated.

'That man who wanted to buy the singing canary – you told him you thought you'd lost the key!'

'Maybe it's around somewhere, like I told him.'

'And the lady who wanted the German doll's house . . .'

'Yes, well, those little holes in the roof just might be woodworm, don't you think? Wouldn't be right to sell damaged goods, now would it?'

'You don't want to sell them, do you?' she persisted.

The clock in the corner of the shop chimed the half-hour.

'Closing time,' said Mr Culpepper. 'Tell you what, we'll lock up and go in the back and have a glass of lemonade, shall we?'

She nodded eagerly, never in a hurry to get home to Aunt Hilda who fussed over her dirty hands or face, or because she had scuffed her sandals or lost her hair ribbon. Aunt Hilda didn't like 'children under her feet', she had explained to Mr Culpepper, and was always pleased when she said she was going out to play. Not that she had any friends to play with, partly because she was new in the village and her contemporaries at school ignored her; but also because Aunt Hilda didn't encourage visiting children nor, indeed, their mothers. It didn't matter any more because she had a friend now – Mr Culpepper.

'Seeing it's the last day of the holidays and you'll not have so much time to come and help me,' he said as he poured lemonade from a jug into two tall glasses, 'I'll explain about the toys. I think you might understand.'

He told her about the orphanage where he'd been taken when he'd been discovered, like Moses in a basket by a stream. 'It was the tenth of February, eighteen hundred and forty, the day our late Queen Victoria – God rest her soul – married Prince Albert.'

199

The child put down her glass and began counting on her fingers. Her violet blue eyes rounded.

'Then you're very very old – as old as some of your toys!'

'Sixty-three next birthday!' he agreed.

'I nearly got sent to an orphanage when Mama died when I was three. Papa has to go to work every day and there was no one to look after me. Then Aunt Hilda said she'd come and live with us so I didn't have to be sent away after all.'

'That's good,' said Mr Culpepper. 'In orphanages – or at least in the one where I grew up – there aren't any toys.'

'Not even at Christmas – or on your birthday?'

'Never on my birthday. Once, one Christmas, a lady came round in a big blue velvet hat with flowers on it – I've never forgotten her. She brought us all toys, one for each of us.'

She sensed his remembered joy.

'So what was your present?'

'A clockwork musical box. It played eight different tunes!'

Her eyes widened still more as she shared his memory. Then he said, 'But we weren't allowed to keep our presents. They were new and very expensive and we were told we might damage them. So they gave us each a threepenny piece instead – to spend on sweets, or a hoop or top, more befitting us orphans. That's when I promised myself that if ever I had the money, I'd buy beautiful expensive toys to make up for the one I couldn't keep.'

'So you did!' she breathed.

200

'Well, not for a long long time. I got a job as a clerk and it wasn't until my fiftieth birthday a relative I'd never known died somewhere in America and left me a small legacy . . . enough to buy this little shop and support me in my old age.'

She smiled happily. 'Tell me the story again,' she said.

'Another day, perhaps. I suppose I did mean to sell the toys but when I bought them, one by one, each of them was a birthday or Christmas present I'd never had as a child . . . so I've kept them and like it or not, I dare say I'll have them now to the day I die!'

'Like my teddy bear,' she said. 'I shall keep it always and always. It belonged to Mama when she was a little girl. That's why he's so old and his fur's so worn.'

'Old is beautiful,' said Mr Culpepper.

When next he saw her, it was a Saturday morning. Autumn winds blew in a shower of crisp brown leaves as she came through the door. Her grey felt winter hat was, predictably, too large for her and her face, paler than ever, was pinched and blotchy with tears. She seemed unable to talk but stood chewing on the white band of hat elastic.

'You're just in time,' he said, tactfully ignoring the threatening tears. 'I've been too busy this morning to oil my engines. Think you could do them for me?'

Her smile reminded him of the sun beaming through his dusty window on an April day.

'Am I old enough? I'll be very careful!'

'Just a drop or two. You'll manage.'

She was so careful, the task took a long time, but eventually, all the engines and even the carriage wheels were oiled.

'Want to tell me what's up?' Mr Culpepper asked as, her job completed, she sat forlornly on the high stool behind the counter. A single tear trickled past the freckles, down her chin and dripped on to the front of her over-large gym slip.

'Aunt Hilda says I'm too old now for a teddy bear. I've become seven, you see, since I last came to visit you. She says I've got to play with sensible toys, like learning to knit or basket weaving . . . and . . . oh, Mr Culpepper, I wouldn't mind so much learning to knit if I could make a jersey for Ted but Aunt Hilda says I'm to give him to the jumble lady when she next calls.'

Her sobs shook the table and a round glass paper weight which filled with snow when shaken, rolled on to the floor. Mr Culpepper picked it up and handed her a large white handkerchief which smelt of engine oil.

'Your papa – he agrees with your Aunt Hilda about the jumble lady?'

'Papa said he understood how I felt but it was really best if I could do what Aunt Hilda wants. When she gets angry, she says she'll go back to Norfolk to live with her sister-in-law like she used to, and Papa says she's only looking after us be- cause it's her duty. He says I must have someone to take care of me or I'd have to be sent away, so we'd best let Ted go . . . and I can't, I just can't. Papa loves him too – because he belonged to Mama and it's all we've got now she's dead. Papa said perhaps that's the trouble – us loving Mama more than we love Aunt Hilda – but I don't see what that has to do with giving Ted to the jumble.'

Mr Culpepper was silent. There were no words to comfort a grieving widower who dared not risk losing his little girl; nor to comfort that little girl who must surrender the toy she loved most in the world.

'Have you thought what it's like to be a teddy bear?' he asked presently. 'Especially if you are a bear who belongs to a girl big enough to go to school all day? He must get very lonely . . . and awfully bored. I mean to say, what is there to look at if you're shut in a nursery cupboard?'

Despite her quiet sobs, he knew by the stillness of her body that she was listening.

'We could sit him in the window – here in my shop!' said Mr Culpepper. 'Between the French Gaultier doll and the kaleidoscope. We could write a card for him, "*circa 1815*" or thereabouts, "*price 4/6d*". You could see him every morning on your way to school and come in and talk to him on your way back.'

'Yes, and you could look after him, Mr Culpepper, and he could watch you doing the oiling and dusting and . . . ' her face creased, 'but . . . but what if someone wanted to buy him?'

Mr Culpepper decided to risk a little joke.

'A moth-eaten old bear like that? Nobody wants moths in their children's nursery!'

Slowly, very slowly, the tear dripped off her chin and, as she smiled, Mr Culpepper was once again reminded of the spring sunshine filling his dusty old shop.

*

So that was the lady's story. She grew up, her aunt went back to Norfolk and eventually the girl fell in love with a young man, rich enough to take care of her and her father. For fifteen years she and Mr Culpepper wrote to each other. Every summer she travelled down from Scotland to see him — and that old bear of her Mama's. She wouldn't remove him because Mr Culpepper had grown very fond of him and said he reminded him of the days they'd spent together in the shop. As far as I know, the teddy bear remained all those years in the window until that day she came to collect him. The old man's solicitor had written to her, you see, explaining that his client had died and what was in his will. Bill and me found it hard to believe that beautiful young woman had ever been the plain, freckled, lonely little girl old Mr Culpepper had befriended. But it made sense later when we packaged the last of the toys into one of the crates and wrote out the label the way we'd been told. 'For the children of St Matthew's Orphanage, wishing you all a Happy Christmas, from Thomas P. Culpepper.'

Since then, I've thought as how, being antiques like, each one of those toys was worth a fair old bit and I've often wondered if they were safe in the hands of those orphans. Bill thinks that some of the kids, unlike Mr Thomas P. Culpepper, might have preferred to receive the equivalent of a threepenny bit.

When we are on one of the long distance removals, Bill and me get to talking about that job. The day after we'd done it, the boss told us that the lady we'd seen was the new owner and he reckoned the old man had left her the toys as well as the shop. The boss had them insured for hundreds of pounds and Bill says if they'd been hers, she would most likely have sold them; that even if she was as well off as she'd looked, you can never have too much.

204

*But I reckon she knew that Mr Culpepper wanted the
kids to have those toys, and it was her as decided to give
them to the orphans.*

   *One thing's for sure — we'll never know the answers,
but it makes you wonder, doesn't it. What do you think?*

A True Story

It was a warm spring afternoon and they were lying in the long grass down by the stream. Across the water, the bees were busy in the golden king-cups and their buzzing made the quiet of the afternoon even more drowsy.

It seemed strange to them both that there were no children for whom they must watch out. Their offspring had long since gone their own ways. Now there were just the two of them. Looking back, there had never been a time when they hadn't been devoted. The first time they had met, they'd been scarcely grown-up, but from that first meeting until now, neither had looked at another with the eyes of love.

There weren't many couples who could say as much; not so many human beings in the world who could with truth call themselves so devoted, so single-minded in their care for one another. They shared everything; home, the garden and, so long as they were young and in need, the children. Now they had only each other.

There was no warning of disaster; nothing to give either of them an inkling of the danger concealed near by. When the stranger attacked, it was too late to get away and there was nothing she could do to help her husband as he rushed forward to defend her. For a moment she stood helpless, panic-stricken, and then she started to run. If she could only reach the house in time, she could get help. Her feet felt like clumsy lumps of lead. She flew rather than ran, in her haste.

At last she reached the house. Inside, Mrs Trower had the washing machine on and the noise drowned her cries. She called louder and beat against the locked door. After what seemed an eternity, the door opened and Mrs Trower said, 'Why, whatever is the matter? Calm down, duck, and tell me what's wrong. My, you are in a state!'

But she couldn't speak. Her terror was such as to render her voiceless.

Mrs Trower seemed to understand her and without stopping to switch off the machine, she followed her back across the garden, through the field and down to the stream.

He lay on the far side, the blood seeping into the crystal water, staining it red. Mrs Trower threw up her hands and gave one cry. Then wading through the water, she bent tenderly over the inert body.

'He's still breathing. Whatever happened?'

At that moment, a huge black mongrel, half Alsatian, half Great Dane, slunk away through the brambles. As Mrs Trower reached for a heavy glistening stone from the bed of the stream, he turned and ran. As he did so, she caught the glimpse of blood against the matted dark coat.

'You brute, you brute!' she yelled after him. Then she turned back to the body.

'He's not dead!' she said with relief. 'But he's badly hurt. We must get him back to the house quickly.'

Much later, Mrs Trower sat down to a cup of tea with her neighbour.

210

'Fair gave me a turn!' she said. 'I've only got the two of them – had them since she first started laying, and I wouldn't have wanted to lose that drake – nor her either. Would you believe it, Mavis, she came all the way back to me for help. True love – that's what I call it. And I've always said ducks are such silly creatures! Yet she showed me as plain as plain she wanted me to follow her. Kept on quacking 'til I did so! Just fancy that!'

Two weeks later, the stiffness had left him and the feathers were beginning to grow again to hide the ugly gashes in his neck and wing. Tenderly, his wife fussed over him but today he was no longer willing for her to lead while he hobbled after. He spread his wings and flapped them and then, a pace or two ahead of her, began the long walk down to the stream.

Without a word being spoken, she knew that the time had come to start another family. And with such a husband to guard her from surprise attacks, she knew she could safely build her nest and hatch out their young. Meekly, obediently, lovingly she followed in his wake until, once more, they lay in the warm sunshine beside the stream.

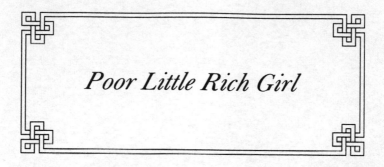

Poor Little Rich Girl

At any other time, the apple loft was one of Elizabeth's very favourite places to be. But this afternoon, her grief was so overwhelming that her senses could encompass nothing beyond the agony and misery that enveloped her.

For a long while, she lay full-length on the rough, dusty boards, her face buried on her bare, folded arms, salty tears cascading down her cheeks and dropping from the tip of her nose amongst the brown, crinkled remains of last summer's store of apples.

How happy she had been the day she and Father had carried the heavy baskets into the barn! One by one 'so that they won't get bruised', Father had cautioned as he had handed them up to her to place in neat rows like lines of soldiers on parade. When the last apple was in position, Father had climbed the ladder to inspect her work.

'You've made a good job of it, Lizzie!' he said in his slow, quiet voice. 'As good a job as I would have done myself!'

How proud she had been! Father never said anything very . . . well . . . *particular*, but she knew by the tone of his voice that he was pleased. Come to think of it, Father never spoke much about anything; but when he did, Elizabeth always listened carefully. She could tell by the way he said things if he was happy or sad, pleased or angry or just . . . just trying to say something to please Mother . . .

215

'I hate her!'

The outrageousness of her own despairing cry shocked her sufficiently to check her sobs. She sat up, rubbing her eyes with grubby fists and smearing her face with dirty streaks. Her cotton frock, she noticed, was also dirty; and torn, too. Mother would be furious . . .

The tears ceased altogether as she remembered that in future there would be no Elizabeth at home for Mother to be furious with. *She had run away.*

'I'll never go back!' she thought. 'Not as long as I live!'

This thought led to another. Would she go back if she died? As a ghost? To haunt them? How frightened silly old Harriet would be! And how sad Mother would be! How sorry for all the cruel, hurtful, cross things she had said to Elizabeth! How she would cry and wish she had been nicer to her poor little daughter before she died.

Had they missed her yet? How long had she been gone? An hour? Maybe more! It must be nearly tea-time and They'd be certain to miss her then. If only she had her watch she would know what the time was. But she had torn it off her wrist, hating it the way she had always hated it since last Christmas when Mother had let Harriet have the one she, Elizabeth, wanted – the one with the red strap.

'Harriet's the oldest so she has a right to first choice!'

Huh! thought Elizabeth. Being oldest had nothing to do with it. The simple truth was that Mother loved Harriet dearly whereas . . .

The tears began to fill her eyes but this time she

did not give way to them. This was her moment of glory; her moment of revenge. Soon They would start calling for her. At first They would not be too worried because They expected her to be late for meals or up to mischief. But after a while . . . when They realized she wasn't anywhere to be found – not in the dog kennel or up the oak tree or bothering Cook in the kitchen – then They would start getting anxious. Mother's face would frown and she'd say to Harriet, 'Run and look in the shrubbery, darling. She's probably hiding . . . just to *vex* me!' Mother always thought she did things especially to vex her. And it wasn't true. If she tore her dress or got lost at the seaside or spilt her cocoa it was only because she was in a hurry or thinking of something else or . . .

'Eee..liz..a..beth!'

She caught her breath. That was Harriet's voice calling her. Harriet had a soft, pretty voice. She never lost her temper or shouted or got angry. Mother said Harriet had the most soothing voice of anyone she knew.

'..liz..a..beth!'

A smile began in her eyes, crinkled her cheeks and spread to her mouth.

They could call as long as they wanted. She wouldn't answer . . . not ever. Later – well, quite soon now – she would start on her journey; just as soon as she had made up her mind where to run away to. The apple loft was just a stopping place, somewhere to finish her cry and decide whether she could risk leaving a farewell letter to Father.

Tears pricked her eyes again. Father would be very unhappy. There was no getting away from it.

217

But for Father, she would have run away years and years ago. But if she left a note for him telling him not to worry about her because she was quite old enough now she was ten to take care of herself, she couldn't be certain he wouldn't tell Mother. And one of the reasons for running away in the first place was to make Mother worry about her and wish she'd loved her youngest daughter even half as much as she loved Harriet.

She suddenly realized that Harriet had stopped calling. She'd probably gone back up the garden to have tea under the beech tree with Mother. She thought of the big glasses of cold, creamy milk, the tiny three-cornered sandwiches and the rich, layered chocolate cake Cook had been icing this morning, and her mouth watered unbearably. She became aware of the intense heat of the apple loft as the late afternoon sun beat down on the timbered roof of the barn. She could see four great columns of hot, golden sun pouring through the window panes below her, the dust swirling about in the beams, shimmering. A big greeny-black bluebottle lay on its back on the window ledge, its feet crossed in death. It was baked dry. If it had been an ordinary day, she would have found a matchbox to put it in and given it a real burial in her animal cemetery with flower petals and prayers. Now, she thought, it will never be buried and she felt sad.

She also felt lonely. The waiting was longer than she had expected. Surely They must have finished tea by now? Where was everybody? Why hadn't They missed her? If someone did not miss her soon, it would be evening and then night and she did not want to begin her journey at night time.

Supposing no one came? Not ever! She could starve to death up in the apple loft and it might be years and years before anyone found her body – dried up like the bluebottle's.

She lay on her back and crossed her arms, trying to imagine what it must feel like to be dead. But the bare rough boards tickled her calves and the backs of her arms and no matter how hard she tried to keep as still as a corpse, she had to sit up to scratch herself.

Moreover, a horrible thought had begun to nag in her head and refused to be kept at bay. *No one was calling out to her* because *no one* cared that she was gone. Harriet certainly wouldn't care. She never minded about anything. All Harriet ever said when things went wrong was, 'Oh, well, it doesn't *really* matter!' which was about the stupidest thing anyone could say when everything mattered very very much to Elizabeth.

As for Mother . . . well, she was probably *glad* Elizabeth was gone.

'Why do you always spoil everything, Elizabeth? I just don't understand you. If Harriet can keep her dress clean, why can't you?' 'I just don't see how you can bear to touch it, let alone want a frog on your bed. It's quite disgusting, Elizabeth, and the fact that it's got a broken leg only makes it worse. You know I've forbidden you to keep any live thing in the house.' 'If you argue *once* more, Elizabeth, I shall have to send you to your room again.' 'Oh, *Elizabeth*, my very best vase! You could have put those wretched bluebells in a jamjar. I don't care if they were supposed to be a present, you know I've forbidden you to touch my Venetian glass . . . '

219

Yes, Mother would be glad to be rid of her. She wasn't at all the sort of daughter Mother wanted. If she'd been like Harriet . . . Harriet was like Mother, dainty, pretty, delicate . . .

She was crying again. This time, the tears would not be checked. She was crying because, like everything else she did, even the plan to run away had gone wrong. Nobody would ever find her and nothing – no one – would ever force her to eat her pride and go back, unasked, unwanted, unloved . . .

The footsteps came closer. Between gulps, she held her breath listening. They were too heavy to be Harriet's. The gardener's? But he went home at tea-time. Nevertheless, it was a man. He came into the barn and began to rummage on the dusty shelf.

Elizabeth craned her neck for a better look. One of the withered apples rolled off the edge of the loft and plopped down by the man's foot. He looked up.

'Hullo, Liz! What are you doing up there?'

It was Father. Elizabeth's heart missed a beat.

'I . . . I've run away!' she gasped.

'Hmm!' said Father, still rummaging. 'I'm looking for that old creosote brush, Liz. I thought I'd give the summerhouse a coat. As a matter of fact, I've been wondering where you were. I thought you'd lend me a hand!'

She scrambled down the ladder and helped him search for the old distemper brush. Her heart was still thumping hard. She *loved* creosoting. She *loved* helping Father. Most of all she loved the thought that Father *needed* her help.

'After all, Liz,' he often said, 'there isn't a boy in this family so you'll have to do instead, so up you go . . . ' as he lifted her into the apple tree, or 'take this brush!' or 'hold that piece of wood for me!' No matter what it was, Father took it for granted she could manage as well as any boy. 'Should've been one!' Father often said, smiling. Oh, how much she loved him.

'There it is!' she cried, handing him the brush. But she made no move to follow him out of the barn.

'Not coming then?' he asked, giving the tear-streaked face a quick look and away again.

'I . . . I *can't*!' Elizabeth wailed. 'I've run away!'

'Hmm!' Father took a long time considering this statement. Before saying anything, he handed her his handkerchief to blow her nose.

'Couldn't you do that some other time?' he said presently. 'I mean, after we've done the creosoting!'

She wanted to laugh but tears came instead and she ran to him and clung to his waist. He didn't put his arms round her because . . . well, because he just wasn't the sort of person who could hug anyone, but she knew he was listening. She told him between sobs about the bluebells that were to have been a surprise for Mother – blue flowers just *belonged* in the blue vase and . . .

'Yes, well, I see!' Father said, giving her his handkerchief a second time.

'I hate her. I *hate* her!' Elizabeth wailed.

Father was very quiet.

'No! No, you love her!' he said. 'And you know, Liz, she loves you. It's just that . . . well, Mother is . . . she doesn't always . . . '

221

They stood side by side in silence. Elizabeth's tears had dried on her cheeks. She wasn't really disappointed. She'd always known – ever since she could remember – that Father would never say anything nasty to or about Mother, no matter what *she* said or did. He loved Mother too much – even more than he loved Elizabeth; even though she was often not at all kind or nice to him! There'd been so many times when she listened to Mother's voice, irritated, cold, critical, talking to Father as if . . . well, as if she didn't love him at all. Yet Father never spoke an angry or an unkind word back, but stood perfectly still, looking . . . looking . . . so she, Elizabeth, had to turn away because she couldn't bear it.

'Don't upset her!' Father said into the silence. 'She . . . hasn't been too well . . . it would upset her . . . and . . . '

As the hopelessly inarticulate man tried to articulate, his face suddenly turned red. In a rush of words, he said, 'We can't run away, Liz. Loving someone the way you and I love Mother is something we'd take with us wherever we ran to. We couldn't just leave her any more than we can stop loving her. The only thing to do is stay near her and try to . . . to please her!'

It was so surprising to hear him say so much in one single sentence, Elizabeth only half listened to the meaning.

'You're probably too young to understand!' Father said as if he was sorry he'd said anything at all.

Perhaps she was. Somehow it didn't really matter. Father had talked to her as if – as if she were grown-up. More important, he'd talked as if the two of them were bound together by the same problem. We. Father and her. Now she came to think of it, it was quite true. Father was as often in trouble as she, Elizabeth. He couldn't do anything right either.

'But will she *ever* love us?' Elizabeth cried.

'Of course she will – and does!' father said.

But he knew there was no hope for the child. She was far too like him.

Progress

It was market day, so the bar of the Four Crowns was crowded. Rosie's arm ached from pulling pints but she was not really aware of it because she was trying to hear the snatches of conversation.

'Won't be no village left the way things are going . . .' John Simms, who owned Sheepdown Farm was saying. 'Oughtn't to be allowed, I say!'

Well, he would feel that way, Rosie thought as she handed a foaming pint to Bill Withers, the smithy. His granddaughter was getting married in the spring and she had been hoping she could buy one of the four cottages that were up for sale in Oakbrook Green.

' . . . pricing our young 'uns out of the market, that's what!' said Bill.

'Two hundred thousand pounds – that's close on a quarter of a million. It's madness!' Ron, the milkman announced.

'Mind you, the cottages will convert easily enough into one house,' Jack Clark, the builder, said knowingly. He, after all, was going to do the conversion and consequently knew more about the newcomers than anyone in the village. He'd had several meetings with the young city gentleman from London who had bought numbers 1-4 Rose Cottages.

'All right for you, Clarky. Keep your lads busy and earn you a bob or two!' John Simms' voice was edged with disapproval and, Rosie thought, a tinge of envy.

Jack flushed.

'What's done's done!' he said defensively. 'I don't approve no more than the rest of you, of Londoners buying up our village. The young man was in no doubt I wasn't keen to do the job . . . said my estimate was far too high.'

Ron gave a loud guffaw.

'No wonder! But he didn't turn it down, did he? You'll soon be that rich, you'll be paying all our pensions, I shouldn't wonder.'

'So why shouldn't I put up my prices? He can afford them. His missus works too: some high-powered job on telly, I think he said, and there're no kids so they can have what they fancy.'

'Let's hope they fancy a pint or two here!' Rosie said, adding glumly, 'although that lot drink in their own homes – champagne probably.'

'Better get some bubbly in stock, Rosie!'

'No, she'd bettern't' broke in old Jones who was, so far as they all knew, close on ninety and the oldest resident in Oakbrook Green. 'Next thing Rosie'll 'ave us lot back in the public bar and us won't be sitting comfortable like in 'ere!'

There was half-hearted laughter from those standing near enough to hear his comment. It struck too near the bone. Before they all knew it, their comfortable day-to-day life would be changing in more than one respect and they didn't want it changed. It was their village and they weren't having foreigners taking it over – 'no more'n we'd 'ave let them Nazis invade us', old Jones had once put it succinctly.

228

'It's that dratted motorway!' Ron said. 'That's what started it all!'

The men were back now to the subject of politics which didn't interest Rosie. Her husband was always on about what a splendid prime minister Mrs Thatcher had turned out to be; how the Four Crowns had been going steadily deeper into the red before the Iron Lady took over and folk had a bit more money to spend; how the bar had been deserted until news of the motorway had brought the men flocking to the obvious meeting place to discuss things. Then there'd been the petition – deciding on how to word it and getting everyone to sign; more meetings in the bar; arguments, heated enough, about the council failing to stop the purchase of farms and land where the motorway was to be built, and finally more meetings when the two rich Londoners put in their bid at the auction of 1-4, Rose Cottages.

Rosie sighed as she dumped some dirty beer mugs into the sink. Business was business and as her old man said, they were back in the blue and if trade continued as it had this past year, they'd get the mortgage paid off. But she could do with some help. Trouble was, most of the young girls were off on the morning bus to Berrytown earning good money as cashiers in the supermarkets or as hairdressers or shop assistants. There was only poor Kirsty unemployed, and she wasn't the type to make a good barmaid; too quiet and shy and nothing to look at. The young men liked a pretty face and a joke or two.

It was a wonder Kirsty had ever got herself in the family way, Rosie thought, echoing the general opinion of all the womenfolk in Oakbrook Green. Never did tell anyone who the father was but suddenly there was Kirsty, size of a house and having a baby in the back bedroom without a word to a soul. Talk of the village it was, at the time; the older women saying her dad, poor man, ought to turn her out, and the younger ones saying there were lots of unmarried mums these days and anyway, Kirsty's dad was a widower and needed her to keep house for him.

Rosie saw Kirsty once a week when she went into the post office to get her child allowance and her dad's pension. Not that they spoke; Kirsty kept herself to herself, but the child – she was nearly five now – was always clean and nicely turned out and so pretty everyone wondered how poor plain Kirsty could have produced her. Only sixteen she'd been when she'd got pregnant. Rosie felt sorry for her, having to stay home to look after the kid when all the girls she'd been to school with had boyfriends or were getting married or finding themselves jobs and earning money to buy smart new clothes and such. Kirsty looked as if all her clothes came from Oxfam.

Kirsty did buy her clothes, such as they were, from jumble stalls, or once in a while, from Oxfam. She didn't care what she looked like and she wanted what little money she had to dress Alison decently. The villagers might look down on her but they weren't ever going to be able to disparage her Alison, not ever.

That Thursday, as she ironed some of her daughter's dresses, there was a smile at the edge of Kirsty's mouth. Had Rosie seen her at that

230

moment, she might have been astonished to realize that beneath the wispy home-cut hair was a pale but charming little face and a sparkle in the dark brown eyes that belied the adjectives 'poor plain Kirsty'! She wasn't feeling poor because soon – only a few more months to wait – she would be rich . . . . rich beyond her imaginings.

Ever since Alison had been born, the only money she'd ever earned was three pounds for a morning's work cleaning at the vicarage. She agreed with her dad that she was being grossly underpaid but she knew the vicar couldn't afford to give her more money. His wife was a semi-invalid and the house was always in a dreadful mess. Sometimes Kirsty stayed on an extra hour or two without pay just to get the place tidied up a bit more.

'Weak in the head, you are, my girl!' her dad said when she was late home from work. 'No wonder you got yourself in the family way!'

Kirsty had hardened herself to his criticism. Maybe she wasn't very bright but nothing – nobody – would ever make her regret having Alison. She was worth all Dad's unkind reminders; all the cold-shouldering she got from the older women in the village and the pitying looks she had from the girls who didn't have any responsibilities.

'Reckon Vicar says you'll get your reward in Heaven – and a fat lot of good that'll do you – or the kid!' Dad had said in one of his sour moods.

No, not in Heaven, Kirsty told herself as she ironed carefully round the tiny pink frill of Alison's best dress, but here, soon, in Oakbrook Green village. She hugged her secret to her. There'd be time enough to tell Dad when the Londoners moved in. Meanwhile, she could think about that day when she'd called in at the post office for her child allowance and old Mrs Harrow had said, 'That young lady from London was in yesterday. Wanted to know if I could tell her the name of a girl in the village who'd clean for them when they moved in. Weren't none, I told her, 'cepting you, and you couldn't take on a full-time job, not with the kiddy to take care of.'

She'd sniffed and shrugged her shoulders, and added, 'Said she wouldn't mind about you taking Alison to work with you. Said she'd call and see you next weekend when they come down to see what progress Jack Clark's been making.'

Kirsty had prayed for several miracles; first that the London lady would indeed call to see her; second that she'd not have found anyone else willing to do the work; and lastly, that if she did call, Alison would be on her best behaviour and not make the lady change her mind.

She didn't expect to like her possible employer – not if the village gossip as to how rich Londoners lived and dressed and behaved was anything to go by.

Village gossip, as usual, proved unfounded. At the weekend Kirsty had opened the door to a pretty blonde woman.

'You must call me Penny!' she'd said. 'My real name's Penelope but I can't stand that. What a beautiful child!' She'd started to make a fuss of Alison and then laughed and said she was wasting Kirsty's time; they must discuss hours and wages, and would four pounds an hour be all right? She was wearing jeans and a baggy white sweater and

232

there wasn't a single piece of jewellery on her.

'Forgive me for being personal!' she'd said; 'but I can't help noticing how spotless your cottage is. I'm sure you'll be just the person I'm looking for, Kirsty. You don't mind if I call you by your first name?' Kirsty shook her head. 'Then can we say it's all settled, subject to satisfactory references, of course? The lady at the post office said you did one morning a week for the vicar's wife, although she didn't say *what* you did! And of course I couldn't expect you to give that up.' She'd laughed and Kirsty had smiled and Alison had giggled, and next thing, Kirsty was promising five days a week and Penny had driven away.

'So Vicar gave you a good reference, did he?' Dad asked a week or two later when Kirsty received Penny's letter confirming her future employment. 'Least he could do, after all you have done for them!'

'He called me "a treasure"!' Kirsty had told him proudly. 'Nobody's called me that in my whole life!'

Word had got out, of course, though Kirsty wasn't sure how. She suspected Penny might have told Mrs Harrow who was the biggest gossip in the village. Now everyone knew, and disapproved, according to Dad.

'No one wants *them* here,' he said. 'You signed that petition same as I did and they all say you've gone over to the enemy just for the money.'

'I need the money,' Kirsty retorted, surprised how often she was standing up to her father these days. It was as if she had suddenly discovered she did have a value after all. 'As to going over to the

233

enemy, people in this village haven't exactly been friendly to me, have they? Anyway, Penny's nice. I like her. I know I'll like working for her.'

'You were born stupid!' said her father, but for once, Kirsty didn't mind.

Down at the Four Crowns, Kirsty's father was on the defensive.

'Clarky's making a packet out of *them* – so why shouldn't *my* Kirsty?' he argued. 'She's got the kid to support, hasn't she?'

The men acknowledged the logic of this remark.

'All the same,' Ron said, 'the rest of us have got to stand firm. We can't stop 'em coming but we can make it plain how we all feel.'

'Can't refuse to serve them,' Rosie's husband muttered. 'Isn't legal!'

'So we do what we have to, but just don't let them feel part of our village,' Ron insisted, waving his beer mug in front of him. 'Sort of give them the cold shoulder – don't buy 'em a pint, talk to 'em – that sort of thing. What d'you say, Bill?'

Bill nodded but said nothing. He was in a bit of a quandary. For years now he'd had a job to make ends meet. There were fewer and fewer horses needed shoeing, no farm implements to mend. He was still five years short of retirement age and yet his capital had dwindled to nothing. Nobody wanted to buy the old forge, leastways not as a business; but ten days back, he'd been in town and one of the big estate agents had approached him.

'If ever you think of selling, Mr Withers, be sure and let me know. I could get you one and a half, maybe two hundred thousand pounds for

234

your place. Several good clients on my books just waiting for a place like yours to convert.'

It was disturbingly and dangerously tempting. Only two things had prevented him saying he'd sell there and then – the furore he knew there'd be in Oakbrook Green, and the fact that as far back down the generations as he could think, Witherses had been the village blacksmiths.

'Of course we'll sell up!' his wife had said. 'You get on that telephone right this minute, Bill Withers, and strike whilst the iron's hot!'

He gave a sour grin at the memory of his wife's choice of words. Apt enough for a blacksmith!

'Don't know what you find so funny about it, Bill!' Ron said as he pushed a full mug in his direction. 'Can't you see what's happening? A year ago we were all united. "Save Our Village". Remember the campaign? And what's happening now, I ask you?'

The bar had fallen strangely silent as Ron's voice rose in volume.

'Well, I'll tell you what's happened. Clarky here's busy making Rose Cottages habitable for *them*; Kirsty's going to clean up for 'em; young Mike's going to deliver papers to 'em; John's going to keep 'em in eggs and cream and fresh chickens and I don't know what else, and Rosie's going to stock 'em up with booze. Next thing we'll have Bill here making wrought iron gates for 'em! So who's united, I want to know? Will one of you tell me that!'

The silence was almost tangible. It was now or never, Bill thought. Deep inside, he knew he was going to sell. He'd be sad in one way but with that kind of money in the bank, he and Betty could do what they'd always wanted – go on a cruise round the world. Then they'd come home and live near their married daughter in Wales. They'd had a good life in Oakbrook Green but neither of them would be that heartbroken at leaving.

Village life wasn't the same any more, no matter how hard folk like Ron were trying to keep it that way. The school had been closed long since and there was talk of the post office licence being withdrawn as all but the old people used the big post office in Berrytown when they went in to shop at the supermarkets.

It was sad, in one way – the end of village life. But you couldn't halt progress any more than they'd been able to stop the motorway coming, or, in his father's day, the replacement of horse transport with cars, sailing ships with steam.

In a minute, when he'd lit his pipe, he'd try to explain things to Ron, try to make him understand why things had to change and villages like Oakbrook Green couldn't exist as they had in his childhood, in his father's day. He felt a sharp pang of nostalgia, remembering the warm moist smell of the shire horses, the shiny bald pate of his father bent over the patiently held, up-turned hooves, the hiss of the hot metal as the iron was plunged into the water to cool. He could see in his mind's eye his mother in her apron, standing in the doorway smiling as she called him in for his tea: freshly baked bread, newly churned yellow butter and mouth-watering home-made gooseberry jam.

He coughed to clear the lump that had risen in his throat.

'See here, Ron,' he said, 'it's like this – things have to change whether we like it or not. It's the same in other countries. Everything's changing all the time. That's what progress is, see? We have to have it!'

'Why?' asked Ron.

Bill sighed. Trust old Ron to ask the one question for which he had no reply.

'Oh, I were all for it – right from the start!'

Ron's voice rang with the conviction of the converted, and grinning, Kirsty nudged her husband's arm. Last spring, she'd married Jeff Barratt, the groom Penny employed to look after her horses, and they lived in one of the houses on the new council estate on the Berrytown road.

Ron, recognized as the oldest inhabitant of Oakbrook Green now that the Joneses had gone, was being interviewed by a television reporter in the saloon bar of the Four Crowns. With a clutch of empty beer mugs in front of him, courtesy of the BBC, he was becoming increasingly voluble.

'Of course, not everyone could see good would come of the motorway. There were plenty who had things to say when they held committee meetings for the "Save Our Village" campaign!' Ron nodded vigorously as if to emphasize the shortsightedness of his neighbours. 'But they's all come round in the end.'

The reporter held his tape recorder closer to the old man's mouth.

237

'You told us you would be seventy-five years old next birthday, Ron. You must have seen a great many changes in your lifetime. It's surprising as well as laudable, that with the wisdom of old age, you yourself could always see the advantages of progress. During the research we have done in other country villages, we haven't always found so enlightened an attitude.'

'Aye, well . . . ' Ron scratched his head and decided to ignore these long words and change the subject.

'So you'll be down with your cameras, like, next Thursday?' he asked. 'And I'll be on the telly for sure?'

As Kirsty stood up to take out the can of Pepsi and packet of crisps she had bought for the waiting Alison, her husband said affectionately, 'What are you grinning at now, love?'

'You'd know well enough, Jeff Barratt, if you'd been sitting in that chair in this pub a year ago. Signing a petition they were, "to keep the enemy out"!' She paused to drop a kiss on her husband's bewildered face and smiled as she glanced back at Ron. 'Ah well, village isn't only thing that's changed. Seems progress can change people's memories, too!'

Still smiling, she went out to the new children's play garden to call her daughter down from the swings.

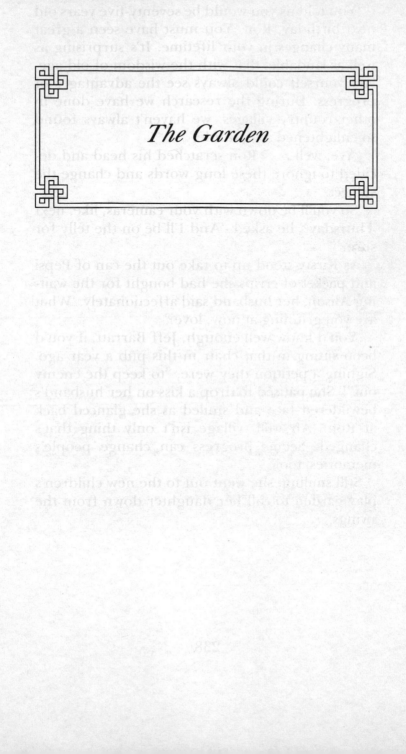

The Garden

Somewhere in the garden the children were playing. From her bed she could hear them but she could not see them. She thought there were five voices but she could not be certain. If only they would come closer to the house – close enough for her to see their faces . . .

A butterfly fluttered against the glass panes of the window, fighting a lone, tenacious battle to reach the sunshine outside, unaware that both mullioned casements were open and that freedom was only an inch away. If she could move she would help it, but instead she could only lie and watch its feeble efforts to escape. Like herself, it too was a prisoner in this room, she thought.

The sun's warmth lay across her white, transparent hands. How thin they were! The blue veins were like lacing beneath the skin. The children were still calling to one another but too far away for her to identify their voices. *If only they would come a little closer* . . .

The rose bushes beneath her window were giving off a sweet, pungent scent. That morning the old gardener, Gatton, had sent up a fragrant bunch of pale yellow blooms, the petals only partly unfurled and still wet with the morning dew. Sister Tindel had arranged them in a cut glass vase and placed them on the table, beside the medicine bottles and boxes of pills.

Was it just a coincidence that Gatton had chosen

her favourite flowers? Or had he guessed who she was?

The birds had quietened, their morning chattering stilled by the heat of the afternoon sun. Only an occasional wood pigeon called from the spinney. The swallows, though silent, remained hard at work, weaving gracefully in wide circles, searching for food in the cool shadows of the trees. They would be down by the lake, too, dipping low over the sparkling water to catch the tiny insects lying on the surface. Soon they would be migrating, but now they were making the most of a rare and perfect English summer.

But the children were not down by the lake. Their voices came from the herbaceous border in which Gatton grew his beautiful, blue delphiniums, red hot pokers, arum lilies and golden rod in a wild profusion of colour. The garden was a perfect place for hide-and-seek. Tomorrow she would insist upon Sister Tindel wheeling her on to the terrace from where she could talk to old Gatton. He must be well over seventy by now.

Tinsel would try to dissuade her from leaving her bed, she thought. A faint smile hovered at the corners of her eyes and mouth. Her starched, efficient nurse/companion disapproved of a great many things – not least of the nickname, Tinsel. Certainly it did not suit her. No one could less resemble the sparkling strands with which the Christmas tree used to be decorated.

Poor Sister Tinsel! How she had hated being dragged away from her beloved California to live in a remote English country house, pandering to the crazy whim of her employer. Perhaps she should have told Tinsel the real reason why she had come to *this* house, *this* garden. But kind, loyal and proficient though Tinsel was, she believed only what she could see and hear or what were proven facts.

But Tinsel deserved to be told the truth. One day she must try to explain. Soon, perhaps.

'Butterfingers!'

There could be no doubt about it — that was Dick's voice. It had to be. It was his favourite expression. Someone must have missed an easy catch, she thought with a smile.

She stared out into the slight haze that lay over the sunlit lawns, her heart beating swiftly. Far away in the distance, she could see the children's shadowy forms leaving the garden, running down towards the lake through the rough grass where the wild daffodils grew in the spring.

She lay back against the pillows, her eyes aching from the strain of looking for the children. She might as well sleep for a little while. Once they were down by the lake, it would be hours before they returned. They would probably go across to the island in the rickety old punt and play *Swiss Family Robinson* until it was time for tea.

The window curtains stirred gently in a soft momentary breeze. Her eyes closed and she slept.

'Another cup of tea, Sister?'

Mrs Gatton's voice held just the right shade of respect due to a trained nurse. Despite her first misgivings, the old gardener's wife had now quite taken to Sister Tindel. Albeit warily, they were becoming friends. In the week since her

243

arrival, Sister Tindel's cool stand-offishness had given way to a keen desire to enjoy a good gossip. Mrs Gatton, plump, rosy-cheeked and cheerful, was only too willing to oblige. She was twenty years younger than her husband, which made her and the nurse contemporaries.

'So you didn't live here before the Second World War?' Sister Tindel asked as she accepted a second cup of tea. The two women were sitting opposite one another at the scrubbed, wooden table in the old-fashioned kitchen. The big, black range was unlit and the great, worn flagstones covering the floor helped to keep the room cool.

'Nor more I did!' said Mrs Gatton, blowing on her tea. 'I didn't marry Gatton until 1950. That was when the trustees decided they wouldn't sell the estate immediately but would put in caretakers for a year or two until the bad name the house had got had died down, so to speak.'

'Bad name?' Sister Tindel echoed, leaning forward eagerly.

Mrs Gatton gave a contented little sigh. She could not have aroused more curiosity in her companion.

'Haunted!' she said portentously. She sat back, waiting for the nurse's reaction. She was a little disappointed to see only disbelief there.

'That's something I just don't believe in, Mrs Gatton. I'm a God-fearing woman and I disapprove strongly of those who dabble in spiritualism.'

'That's as may be,' argued Mrs Gatton with a country-woman's stubbornness, *'but things happened.'*

There was a short pause before sheer curiosity drove Sister Tindel to ask, 'What things?'

'Poltergeists!' Mrs Gatton murmured darkly.

'You mean those hobgoblins who break dishes and empty closets and the like?'

'I don't know about hobgoblins,' Mrs Gatton said doubtfully. 'I've never seen naught myself, but the girls as came up from the village to clean before I came here – they said as how brooms were whisked from out of their hands, buckets of water were spilt on the floors, dusters went flying out of windows. And there were wild shrieks as would fair turn your stomach to hear. The girls wouldn't come no more after that.'

'Imagination!' said Sister Tindel firmly. But she leant forward, eager to hear more.

'Them girls weren't the only ones to see and hear things,' Mrs Gatton continued doggedly. 'There were tenants came on a long lease – home from India they was. *They* heard things, too. And they left in a hurry as never was explained. After that the trustees decided to leave the place empty and asked Gatton if he'd stay on to keep the garden tidy, and did he know a woman as would dust round the house and keep it aired. That's when Gatton asked me to marry him so as we could take the position.'

'But *you've* never seen anything strange?' Sister Tindel insisted.

Mrs Gatton shook her head. 'No more I have. But Gatton has. He sees them often – leastways he says he does – but he don't take no notice of 'em.'

'Them?' asked Sister Tindel. 'Who?'

'Why, the children, or so *he* says. Them as used to live here before the war.'

245

Mrs Gatton plugged in the electric kettle to make a fresh pot of tea. Sister Tindel watched her thoughtfully.

'Not that I knew the family but Gatton did. He's been gardener here since he was a boy.' Mrs Gatton warmed to her story and her companion did not interrupt. 'Five children there were. The eldest boy was at Eton when war broke out. He lied about his age and joined up and was blown to pieces at Dunkirk. That was Master Dick.'

She poured boiling water into the big brown teapot.

'Then one of the girls went up to London to drive an ambulance in the Blitz and six months later she was killed. The parents were ever so upset by it but they couldn't give way because they had the others to think about. Then the two youngest children who were away at boarding school and quite safe everyone thought – they was both killed when a stray bomb from a German plane hit the school. And that left only the eldest girl. She was somewhere abroad when the war broke out and never got home to England. She married a foreigner, I believe.'

'And what happened to the parents?' Sister Tindel enquired.

'They didn't neither of them see the war out,' Mrs Gatton said matter-of-factly. 'Gatton says as how they died of broken hearts but it was much more like the Asian flu did it. Dreadful epidemic there was and what with food rationing and the like, people wasn't as healthy as they should have been and they weren't exactly young folk, either.'

At that moment the bell rang. Sister Tindel

246

jumped to her feet. She had quite forgotten her patient.

'It'll be her for her tea!' she exclaimed. 'I said to ring when she'd had her nap. Funny how she's taken to drinking tea now she's back in England. It used to be coffee morning, noon and night in California.'

Mrs Gatton was now brewing a third pot of tea but this time it was in the silver teapot.

'Funny her wanting to come and live in this house,' she mused. 'I mean . . . with her days being numbered, so to speak. How long did the doctors give her?'

'Six months at most the specialist said. But she seems much better since we came here, and I'm wondering if he could have been wrong. Poor soul. For all her money she's had a sad life.'

'It was a motor accident paralysed her, didn't you say?'

Sister Tindel nodded.

'Killed her little girl, Nancy, at the same time. Five years old she was. She doesn't talk about her but she dreams and wakes up crying her eyes out, poor dear. She seems to think the little girl is lonely. Of course, I've told her she shouldn't take dreams seriously, but with her being so ill she's bound to be fanciful.'

'Looks like she was doomed to have bad luck right from the beginning,' Mrs Gatton said with a certain relish. 'She's a widow, didn't you say?'

'Yes. Her husband was killed in the Far East. They'd only been married a couple of months, and I don't think she'd known him long enough to feel it as much as she did when the child was killed.'

247

Sister Tindel lifted the tea-tray and, nodding to Mrs Gatton, left the kitchen to make her way upstairs. Mrs Gatton went to the big pine dresser and took a mug which she filled with tea for old Gatton. He'd be down in the greenhouse tying up tomatoes as like as not. Never stopped working, although there was no one pressing him. Seemed a bit silly to her the way he went on. She reckoned he'd go on tending that garden just for love even if they stopped paying him. Perhaps it made a difference that he'd worked in it since he was fourteen; learned his trade as gardener's boy. There'd been four of them employed in those days, one for the greenhouses, one for the vegetables and one for the lawns and hedges, and Gatton to help where he was needed. She didn't really mind except that it would have saved her legs if he stopped working long enough to come in for his tea.

She picked up the mug and set off down the worn brick path through the garden, knowing that sooner or later she would find him somewhere out there.

'You've been here a long time, haven't you, Gatton?'

'Aye!'

She smiled. Unlike his wife, Gatton used few words. For a minute or two she sat perfectly still. She had made Sister Tindel bring her wheelchair to the edge of the York stone terrace from where she could smell the roses in the beds below. Gatton was stooped over one of the bushes, snipping off dead blooms with his secateurs.

'Will you tell me about them, Gatton?' she said softly.

248

He did not look up from his work but he heard her. He grunted once or twice and then said, 'Five of 'em grew up here. Two lads, three lasses.'

'Yes, I know. Dick was the eldest.'

'Aye!' Still he did not look at her.

'Then Evelyn.'

He turned and stared at her – a long, searching look. Then he went back to his work but his hands were idle and the rose cutters silent.

'Miss Penny, Master Graham and little Miss Anne.'

His voice was so quiet she could barely hear him. For a moment tears blinded her eyes and she could no longer see Gatton's bent back and gnarled hands, or the criss-cross of wrinkles on his brown face.

'It was the war!' Gatton's voice was suddenly angry. 'Aye, that's what it was; the war!'

'Yes,' she agreed. 'But, Gatton, if there had been no war, they couldn't go on being children for ever – like Peter Pan.'

Gatton did not reply. She was not certain if he had ever known of their favourite game; that they had christened the island on the lake Never Never Land – that magic island where from sheer force of their combined wills, they could make time stand still.

'Thought as how Miss Evelyn might come back after the war.'

Was there a question in Gatton's voice?

'But she thought they'd all gone,' she replied. He seemed to understand. She had never imagined they might still be here. What then had made her decide to come home when the doctor had said six months was all he could promise? That was the first time it had crossed her mind that they might still be in the garden.

'Gatton, *how many are there?*' she asked with sudden urgency.

There was a long pause while he gathered up the rose heads and put them carefully into a trug. Then he stood up and looked away from her towards the lake.

'Were four,' he said, more to himself than to her. 'Were four until lately. Now there's another one – but it ain't Miss Evelyn.'

He walked away from her without looking back. She lay with her eyes closed, her heart beating painfully fast. So she had been right when she had seen them on the lawn this morning. Five – and the extra child was a little girl who had Nancy's long, straight, silky fair hair and fat little legs.

A bumble-bee buzzed angrily in one of the rosebushes. The sun was a warm, golden light on the windows of the old house. It was so quiet she could hear a mouse scurrying through the dry grass beneath the terrace. Then she heard a voice, quite close,

'*Don't tease her, Graham. She can't help her accent. It's American.*'

'*We're Best Friends!*'

'*Girls!*'

There was a scuffle, a giggle. Then Dick's voice, beginning to break and unreliable, '*Where's Eve? She's been gone for ages.*'

'*She'll be here soon. M'selle gave her a hundred lines. "I must not be rude to my elders and betters"* . . . *only M'selle spelt rude rood. We nearly died laughing.*'

'*I wish Eve would hurry up. We can't go to the island till she comes.*'

Sister Tindel came out on to the terrace.

'There you are, having a nice little nap. I've brought you a cup of . . . is there anything wrong? You do look pale. Stay there, dear. I'll call Mrs Gatton and we'll soon have you back in bed. There, I said it would be too much for you.'

'Sister Tindel, let me stay . . . I want to stay here . . . I . . .' But her voice would make no sound. Her chest hurt and breathing seemed suddenly difficult. Everything became a little misty.

Gatton came up to her. He laid his gnarled hand on hers and said, 'There, Miss Evelyn. It'll be all right soon, you'll see.'

They lifted her back into her bed and Mrs Gatton went down to the kitchen tut-tutting, while Sister Tindel hurried off to telephone the doctor. The room was quiet again. She still couldn't breathe. Then the door opened and Dick came in. He was laughing.

'*There you are!*' he said. '*I've been looking everywhere for you.*'

He lay down on the floor and began to worm his way under the bed.

'*Dick!*'

'*Sssh! We're playing sardines, idiot. They'll hear you.*'

Presently Anne came, holding Nancy's hand. Anne whispered, '*Nancy's my very best friend, Eve!*'

'*I know!*' she whispered back. Her chest hurt agonizingly, but she didn't mind the pain. Nancy was squeezing under the big red eiderdown and giggling.

'*I like sardines. This sure is fun!*'

251

She hoped Sister Tindel would not come back too soon. She couldn't bear it if they went away without her. It was hot under the bedclothes. She couldn't breathe. Then Graham wriggled in on her far side. He sneezed twice and laughed when Dick called to him, 'Shut up!' The room became quiet again. The door squeaked and it seemed as if she could no longer hold her breath . . . her lungs were bursting.

Penny came in.

'*Found you!*'

They were tumbling about on the bed all around her.

'*Took you long enough!*'

'*Let's hurry. Mother's packed a picnic for us to take on the island, and I've snitched a bunch of grapes from the greenhouse.*'

'*Gatton will be livid!*'

'*Come on, come on!*'

'*Hurry up, Eve!*'

They stood by the open door, looking at her, their arms outstretched. Far away, as if from another world, she heard Tinsel's voice saying, 'Do hurry, Doctor. I think she's had an attack. I wouldn't be surprised if she's going.'

'*Of course I'm going, Tinsel!*' Her voice was suddenly loud. Her breathing was no longer painful. '*We're going to the island for tea.*'

She jumped off the bed and ran past the grown-ups. She'd probably get another hundred lines for pushing. She laughed. Grown-ups never seemed to understand when children were in a hurry.

'*Come on, Eve.*'

'*I'm coming, I'm coming.*'

'Race you to the greenhouse!'

Dick would win, of course. He always did.

Gatton stood, his hands clasped tenderly round a pot of geraniums. He counted the children as their strong, young, sunburnt bodies ran gaily past him. One, two, three, four, five, six . . . yes, *six*.

'I thought so,' he muttered, and with a nod of his head he went back to tending the geranium cuttings that were to replace the old yellow rosebush which had outlived its span.